LALA

The RADs are free, and Lala is flashing he
But when Daddy Drac pays her a surpris
goes batty. Mr D thinks the RADs shoul
school, but Lala isn't ready to give up the rights she and her
friends have fought so hard for. When she hears about a
glamorous contest that awards the winning school mad
moola and starring role in a national ad campaign, Lala
decides to bite. It's father against daughter in a battle for
Salem's student body. Lala is determined to save Merston
High . . . but she might die – twice – trying.

FRANKIE STEIN

Frankie can't believe that Brett betrayed her. Just when she
thought she had sparked a new romance, it seems to have
fizzled out. Still, Frankie is charged up and ready to fight
for her rights. She refuses to run for the hills, and since her
face isn't shown in the video, she can afford to stay in Salem.
Who's with her? . . . Hello? Anyone still here?

MELODY CARVER

Melody wants to help put the smackdown on Bekka's Monster
Home Tours, but she's kinda busy trying to get the truth out of
her parents and keep Ms. J from sending Jackson into hiding. As
she struggles to walk the line between normie and RAD, she starts
to realize that people are actually listening to what she says – even
Candace! Is Melody's newfound voice here to stay?

Fitting in is out.

Also by
LISI HARRISON

Monster High
Monster High
The Ghoul Next Door
Where There's a Wolf, There's a Way

The Clique
The Clique
Best Friends for Never
Revenge of the Wannabes
Invasion of the Boy Snatchers
The Pretty Committee Strikes Back
Dial L for Loser
It's Not Easy Being Mean
Sealed with a Diss

BACK AND DEADER THAN EVER

A novel by

Lisi Harrison

www.atombooks.net

ATOM

First published in the United States in 2012 by Poppy,
an imprint of Little, Brown and Company
First published in Great Britain in 2012 by Atom
Reprinted 2012 (twice), 2013

A CIP catalogue record for this book
is available from the British Library.

ISBN 978-1-907410-66-6

Printed and bound in Great Britain by
Clays Ltd, St Ives plc

Papers used by Atom are from well-managed forests
and other responsible sources.

MIX
Paper from
responsible sources
FSC® C104740

Atom
An imprint of
Little, Brown Book Group
100 Victoria Embankment
London EC4Y 0DY

An Hachette UK Company
www.hachette.co.uk

www.atombooks.net

For Hallie Jones, the ghost-est with the most-est.

A special *merci beaucoup* to Ingrid Vallon,
a wonderful friend and *française* proofreader.
J'adore.
(Ingrid, did I spell all that properly?)

TABLE OF CONTENTS

PROLOGUE
LET'S GET VISIBLE

The invisible charmer had a girlfriend. She was spirited and smelled like lilacs. She loved listening to live bands and reporting "the latest" to gossip-starved students. She held hands with him. She tittered at his jokes. Things were getting serious.

It was time for Billy to wear clothes.

"Prepare to go from zero to hero," Frankie said, holding open the door to Abercrombie & Fitch.

"There's an itch in Fitch, and we're gonna scratch it," Billy added, grinning with anticipation as he stepped into the air-conditioned store. The holiday season had just ended, and thus everything was on sale. High prices were no longer an excuse for nudity. He was ready to zip up, button up, and show up.

"Look," said Frankie, pointing at their reflection in the wood-framed mirror. A green girl with white-streaked black hair, plaid tights, and a denim minidress was standing beside a floating pair of sunglasses and tattered Timberlands. The duo burst out laughing.

In a romantic comedy, this would be a pivotal scene. While watching it, the audience would decide that Billy should be with Frankie instead of the lilac-scented girl. The moviegoers would have seen how they laughed on the train from Salem to Portland. Heard strangers refer to them as a perfect couple. Marveled at how uninhibited they were with each other. And everyone in that audience would long for the person seated beside him or her to be just as dynamic.

But this wasn't a movie. It was real life. And for once, Billy Phaedin's story was more magical than Hollywood.

They sifted through the racks, blissfully unaware of other shoppers and their puzzled glances. Afloat in a bubble of inside jokes and laughter, they hardly noticed a mother pulling her tween daughter closer to her hip.

"Welcome," said a California blond in a ruffled black dress and a bright blue hoodie. She turned to peek at her coworker by the cash register, as if executing a dare. "Can I help you find your size?" And then a little louder, "And your body?"

The girl at the register smacked the counter in disbelief and cracked up. Billy clenched his fists. Frankie had warned him about this. It had taken weeks of shopping in Salem before the salespeople began treating her like a normie. Now she was a VIP. But Voltage Important Person status wasn't granted after a single spree. It took time and trust. And they were in Portland now, breaking into a new market. So Billy bit his lip and let Frankie do the talking.

"We'd love the help," she said, twisting her hair into a knot. *How do girls do that?* Billy wondered. Her bolts gleamed unapologetically. "My friend needs a wardrobe."

"You're not from around here, are you?" asked the girl with a know-it-all squint.

"Salem," Frankie said.

"Thought so. I heard about you guys," she said, eyeing Frankie's bolts. She reached for them. "Are those —?"

Frankie swatted the girl's hand. "Don't touch. They're live."

The blond blushed. "Sorry."

"No prob." Frankie smiled. "You hook Billy up with some mint clothes, and I'll send you a pair of stick-ons from my father's lab. I do it for all my mall friends back home."

"F'real?"

Frankie nodded.

"Epic. Well, I'm Autumn. And if you guys want to have a seat in our dressing lounge, I'll start pulling some looks."

Frankie led the way and Billy followed. Not the way he used to, galumphing like a sad puppy because she was crushing on Brett Redding instead of him. On this day he was more like a proud pony, trotting joyfully because he was the exception to the Hollywood rule. He could have a megawatt-hot best friend and no longer have to fight the urge to kiss her. She could even have a cool normie boyfriend he didn't want to choke. He was that stable.

Ever since he met Spectra—two months earlier at Clawdeen's Sassy Sixteen party—the only thing Billy had felt for Frankie and Brett was happiness. He no longer felt invisible. Spectra and her playful sense of humor, girlie giggle, and just-because kisses brought color and definition to his world in a way that spray tans never could.

They settled into the brown leather couch outside the fitting rooms and helped themselves to the complimentary A&F water.

"Spectra's been begging me to get visible," Billy said, dropping his sunglasses into Frankie's purse. "She's gonna freak."

Frankie took a small sip and then screwed the top back onto her bottle. "She'll probably tell everyone you were just given a full wardrobe as the new spokesmodel for the store."

Billy sighed. *Here we go again.* "Spec may cut corners when it comes to fact-checking, but she's not a liar."

There was a time when Billy would have hoped Frankie was speaking out of jealousy. But he knew better. Frankie might be green on the outside, but inside she was pure gold—except when it came to Spectra's "stories." Those made her see red.

"I'm not saying she's a liar," Frankie insisted. "More like a—"

Billy stiffened. "A what?"

Frankie paused to consider her words. "A verbal free spirit."

"Maybe because she *is* a spirit," he tried.

"I'm talking about her rumors," Frankie insisted. "Half the time it's like she's just making stuff up." And then she added, "I'm sorry," as she always did. "I just don't want you to get hurt."

"I won't," Billy assured her. "Spectra may fill in the blanks sometimes, but she's not mean."

"She could spread a fake rumor about you or—"

A Bieber-haired boy stepped out of the fitting room holding a striped V-neck. He paused to watch Frankie, who appeared to be talking to herself.

"What are you looking at?" Billy asked in his deepest voice. "Never seen a green ventriloquist before?"

"Uh..." The boy scanned the lounge as if looking for hidden cameras. When he didn't find any, he stiffened—and

4

then grinned. He took a step closer and lifted his palm. "Right awn."

Billy thrust his own palm forward and smacked the guy like a long-lost brother. The unexpected force launched Bieber Boy straight into a clothing rack. Hangers swayed wildly above his limp body.

Frankie raced toward him. "Omigod, are you okay? It was an accident. Usually people run away. We're not used to—"

"I'm cool," he grunted, and then wobbled to his feet with the grace of a colossal pregnant woman. "Can I take your picture?"

He didn't seem to mind that one of his subjects was invisible. There was something about the way Frankie's arm seemed to hover in midair that thrilled him into a dozen thank-yous.

"Things are really different now," Billy said once they were alone again. The RADs' growing acceptance was starting to spread beyond Salem.

Frankie twirled a loose wrist seam around her finger. "It's hard to believe Clawdeen's party turned everything around."

"Losing your head at the school dance kind of got the ball rolling, don'tcha think?"

Frankie giggled at the memory. "We're not freaks anymore."

"I know. It sucks." Billy sighed.

Frankie shot him a look.

He smiled. "I have to find new material."

"It's about time."

"Where's my model?" asked Autumn, her arms stacked with stylishly wrinkled plaids and denims.

Billy wiggled his boot. "Here."

"Epic. I'll just put this stuff in a room and—"

"S'okay," Billy said, grabbing half the stack and placing it beside him on the couch. "I can change out here. It's not like anyone can see anything, right?"

Frankie jumped to her feet and clapped. "Fashion show!"

For the next hour, Billy allowed himself to be dressed and undressed by two gorgeous girls who wanted nothing more than to make him as cute as visibly possible. He was out in public owning his RADness, mere hours away from a night of lilac-scented hugs.

And the invisible boy lived happily ever after....

"Just promise me you won't change," Frankie said as they rode the train home, cocooned in a nest of black-and-white bags.

"I promise," he said, but it was too late. He already had.

CHAPTER ONE
GHOULS JUST WANNA HAVE FUN

Frankie triple-checked the date on her iPhone to make sure she wasn't hallucinating. It still read *June 1*. Yellow sparks sprayed from her fingertips, raining down around the crowded bleachers in the school gym. They settled by her black-and-white-striped Mary Janes and then winked out like fireflies. After this day, there would be twenty-three days of school left! Twenty-four days until the first day of summer vacation! Twenty-four days until twenty-four-seven VOLTAGE!

Amid the mounting sounds of chattering students jockeying for seats, the normie boy beside her placed a warm hand on her shoulder. *You okay?* his denim-blue eyes seemed to ask.

Frankie smile-nodded and then returned to the screen. After six months of PDA (public displays of anxiety), Brett Redding still noticed her every flicker. If she sparked during a test, he'd lift his gaze and wink reassuringly. If she sparked when a teacher called on her, he'd place a hand on her back. When she sparked during a scary movie, however, he'd laugh. But Merston High's other students? They had stopped marveling at her quirks months earlier. The shock of seeing Frankenstein's granddaughter snap, crackle, and pop was *soooo* last November.

Unable to sit still, Frankie bounced her mint-green knee. *Zap!* Another spark singed a small hole in the polyurethane coating on the bench. She wrinkled her nose and tried to wave away the smell of burning plastic before anyone noticed.

"What's with the light show?" he asked, scanning the gym for a possible cause.

"I'm fine," Frankie assured him as she thumbed her keypad. "I just thought of something else for my summer to-do-or-die list, and I got excited."

"It's just called a to-do list." Brett grinned. "You know that, right?"

"Not mine." She quickly typed: EXPERIMENT: TAN LEGS ONLY, SO IT LOOKS LIKE I'M WEARING DARK GREEN TIGHTS. "To-dos are a snooze. Everything on my list is to *die* for," Frankie insisted, defending her sixteen ideas. Because, really, they were more than just ideas. They were warm-weather adventures. At least, they were to her. Most of her friends had already tasted the salty Pacific Ocean or spent an entire day barefoot; caught a real firefly in a jar or tried a three-day solar-energy cleanse. But not Frankie. She may have been implanted with fifteen years' worth of knowledge, but this was going to be her first summer of real life. And she was going to seize the season with every stitch in her body. She just had to make it through this last weekly diversity-training assembly without shorting out, and she'd be one hour closer.

Blue squeezed in beside Frankie on the bench. Once settled,

she wound her blond curls up in a knot and secured them with an aqua lacquered chopstick. Fanning the back of her neck, the Aussie sea creature sighed. "Man, I can't wait to don the ol' bathers and soak my scales in the fuzzy."

"What time is your pedicure?" Frankie wondered, thinking she'd benefit from a little piggy polish herself.

"Nay, Sheila," Blue said with her usual dolphin-y cackle. "That was Australian for 'I need a swim.' I'm as chapped as a mozzy in the Woop Woop." Sunbeams shone through the gym's skylight and onto her dry scales, casting iridescent crescent-shaped glimmers on the wall behind them.

"A swim sounds voltage!" Frankie beamed. "Let's get a big group together. I'll have Daddy turn down the turbines in our backyard, and we can jump in the falls."

Blue clapped her pink-mesh-gloved hands for joy.

"What's this I hear about a pool party?" Clawdeen asked, making her way up the steps. She plopped her red leather cross-body bag on the bench beside Blue and then pulled an orange chunk of foam from her right ear. The canine's ears were too sensitive for assembly noise. But social plans and gossip? She never tuned those out. "Where and when?" she asked, removing the left earplug.

"My house after school," Frankie announced.

"Works for me," Clawdeen said, fluffing the auburn tuft around her neck and then jamming the plugs back in place. Even though the moon wasn't close to full, Clawdeen's arms and neck were covered in luxurious fur. She was in perpetual Hollywood glam mode since she had cut back on the waxing and upped the grooming. Normies in every grade were now adorning their collars and sleeves with synthetic pelts in a multitude of textures and colors. Yet none could compete with the shine and fullness of Clawdeen's. She DIYed herself a crystal brooch that said FUR REAL and wore it daily, just in case they tried.

Cleo squeezed in beside Clawdeen. Bodies parted Red Sea–style to let her through. She finger-combed her bangs and then surveyed the crowd. Her purple jersey minidress wrapped her caramel-colored curves like a birthday present; the gold linen strips around her wrists were the bows.

"Is skinny-dipping allowed at this pool party?" Billy asked from somewhere nearby.

"What was the point of all our shopping trips if you're not going to wear your new clothes?" Frankie asked her invisible best friend.

"It's hot out," he said.

"Well, I hope your invisibooty isn't on these benches," Cleo said, sitting. The smell of amber and superiority surrounded her like a protective bubble. "My outfit hasn't been Scotchgarded yet."

"How about beeotch-guarded?" Billy snipped.

Everyone giggled except Cleo's boyfriend, Deuce. He knew better than to laugh at anything that cast his royal girlfriend in an unflattering light. Instead, he began to squirm like the snakes under his beanie, and turned to greet his b-ball buddy Davis Dreyson in the row behind them. Deuce's signature mirrored Ray-Bans reflected his friend's easy smile.

"Why are we even here?" asked Blue. "We're as diverse as a two-headed dingo." She wrapped her arms around Irish Emmy—her new normie friend from the swim team—and then kissed her sloppily on the cheek. "See?"

"Aww, dry up, ya bird." Irish Emmy giggled, wiping the slobber off her pale face. Her flat-ironed red hair undulated like sea grass.

Blue was right. They didn't need lectures and tolerance exercises anymore. The diversity-training assemblies had done a mint job of teaching normies and RADs how to coexist peacefully. There hadn't been a single issue in months. In fact, RAD (Regular Attribute Dodgers) were trending up this semester. Way up.

Frankie's seams had inspired the latest henna tattoo craze: shoulder and wrist stitches. Cleo admirers wrapped their arms in linen. Deuce's signature hat-and-sunglasses look had spread through the basketball team faster than athlete's foot. Faux-fur tributes to Clawdeen rolled down the halls like tumbleweed. And Blue's sleeves were advertised in the latest spring colors. Freak was finally chic. So why not call it a day? An early dismissal for a job well done? After their swim, they could rent a paddleboat and drift along the Willamette River. Breathe the grass-scented air. Sample each flavor of gelato—

"Everyone up!" shouted a frizzy-haired fortysomething as she walk-bounced toward the center of the basketball court. As if working the runway at O'Hare Airport, she waved the students to stand.

Mrs. Foose—the school's "integration expert," as Principal Weeks called her—had been hired to teach tolerance to the students at Merston High. "Maybe she can teach us how to tolerate her wardrobe," Cleo had remarked at the first assembly. And as much as Frankie hated to judge, she could see Cleo's point. Foose's uniform—an oversize slogan tee (today's said LOVE THY

11

GAYBOR), high-waisted Levi's, and teeter-tottering purple-and-silver EasyTone Reeboks—was hard to condone.

"It's our last assembly of the year, so sing it like you mean it." Mrs. Foose pressed a button on her old-school boom box and stiffly lifted her left hand to her chest. A rather robust rendition of Merston High's new anthem echoed through the gym. Frankie—always eager to make the best of a boring situation—stood in the bleachers and sang at the top of her lung space.

> *"Come one, come all, don't hesitate!*
> *At Merston High we tol-er-ate!*
> *Class is cool; let's go study.*
> *High school rocks when a RAD's your buddy!"*

Frankie sang this line extra loud, and everyone applauded and jumped up on the bleachers. Mrs. Foose flashed a thumbs-up, reveling in the surge of teen spirit. Frankie flashed a thumbs-up back. Cleo rolled her topaz-colored eyes, probably wishing she could cut off Frankie's thumb and jam it up her—

> *"Buuuut…normies are quite special too,*
> *So mix and mingle—it's not taboo!*
> *Learn from each other, never smother.*
> *Merston High: It's like no other!"*

Frankie led the school in a round of enthusiastic bleacher stomping while Mrs. Foose wiped tears of pride from her eyes.

"Don't hate!" the teacher called, fist-pumping.

"Tol-er-ate!" the students responded.

12

Applause rang out as Mrs. Foose turned off the boom box and adjusted the microphone on her headset. "Seats, everyone!"

Feedback pierced their restless murmurs. Clawdeen covered her ears.

"Sorry about that, Wolfs!" Mrs. Foose said, assuming her serious stance—hands clasped behind her back, knees locked. "Today marks the final lecture in the Merston High Dive into Diversity program."

Everyone applauded.

She waved them silent, her triceps flapping like sails on the open sea. "When we first met, Merston was divided. RADs"— Mrs. Foose punctuated this with enthusiastic air quotes—"lived in fear and secrecy. Normies"—she air-quoted again—"were dominant."

"Woo-hoo!" a male voice called.

Mrs. Foose clapped sharply and held up her index finger. The student body was one now. "Thanks to your hard work," she continued, "we've had an incredible semester here at Merston. Our swim team, led by Lagoona Blue, went to the state finals for the first time in twenty years."

"Rake!" Irish Emmy fist-bumped Blue.

Frankie patted Blue on the back. Everyone cheered. Blue grinned and wound a stray curl around her forefinger. A bleached blond with eyeliner gills on her neck reached back for a high five.

Mrs. Foose continued. "Coed track made it to the national meet in April thanks to the Wolf family." Clawdeen and her brothers raised both arms above their heads. "And both our basketball and football teams are undefeated." Deuce and Clawd stood and bowed. "This has been an unprecedented season for

Merston High athletics thanks to our RADs and their extraordinary skills."

Applause echoed off the cinder-block walls.

"I look out at you and see appreciation and acceptance," Mrs. Foose went on. "Today I see tomorrow. And it looks like a rainbow, friends. One big, bold rainbow. And if you help me spread this colorful light, soon the whole world will be lit by our love. And you will always know that it started right here. With you. At Merston High!"

Frankie jumped up on the bleachers and stomp-cheered. Once again, everyone followed. Everyone but Cleo. Instead of cheering, she stayed seated on the shaking bench, struggling to apply her gold-flecked lip gloss.

True, she was never one for grand overtures. Normally, Cleo was catlike, expressing her approval with subtle gestures: a measured smile here, an eyelash bat there. But lately—ever since the combined total of Frankie's Facebook and Twitter friends exceeded Cleo's (on May 22, 7:04 PM, 607 versus 598)—she'd been more aloof. Vengeful, even. Frankie had considered cutting back on her tweets and posts. Maybe that way she would lose a few online friends and even the score. Anything to deflect Cleo's snooty comments and unsettling eye rolls—they were the number one side effect of jealousy, her mother had explained. But Brett and Billy had joined forces to talk Frankie out of it. *Why make your virtual friends suffer just because Cleo's status is slipping? You're all-around nicer. No wonder they like you more. What, no one else is allowed to be popular? She should be kissing your bolts, not the other way around.* So Frankie tried to bolster Cleo's royal ego with flattery that usually fell flat.

14

"Hey, Cleo," Frankie called. "If we're in an earthquake, will you do my makeup?"

"Yeah, that'll be the first thing on my mind," she snarled.

Frankie's heart space tightened. It was useless. Everything she did got Cleo's linens in a bunch.

"Ignore her," whispered Spectra, Billy's invisible girlfriend. "Fact: Her twin sister, Nefra, is moving to Alexandria for the summer. Cleo is heartbroken. They, like, sleep in the same sarcophagus and everything. She's just taking it out on you."

"Good to know," Frankie said politely, repressing the urge to roll her eyes. Everyone knew Nefra lived in Cairo and was three years older than Cleo. *Can't Spectra get anything right?*

"Hold your chatter!" Mrs. Foose shouted, silencing the students with another sharp clap. "Our work isn't done yet. We're riding the pendulum too far in the other direction. Normies have been benched during games. They're hiding their natural beauty behind RAD-influenced makeup and accessories—"

"What's wrong with that?" Cleo muttered.

Clawdeen giggled into her palm.

"We need to strike a balance," said Mrs. Foose. "Every color needs to shine before we call ourselves a rainbow."

"Can I get some nachos with that cheese?" whispered Brett. Frankie smile-nudged him, catching a whiff of the wax-scented balm that kept his black hair so perfectly spiked.

"For our final exercise before school lets out for the summer..."

Everyone moaned. Principal Weeks stepped forward and raised his hands for silence. The gym slowly quieted. He nodded for Mrs. Foose to continue.

"I'd like for us to focus on balance. And to do that, each grade must form a Balance Board. It will be equally composed of RADs and normies. For the remainder of this year and into next, team members will be charged with addressing the needs of their fellow students. Social events, facility upgrades, even new classes and sports. Anything and everything that will bring balance to our rainbow."

Surprisingly, several students—especially those in the first few rows—applauded. Mrs. Foose and Principal Weeks exchanged a proud glance.

Bwoop. Bwoop.

Yes! The day had finally ended. It was time to swim! The bleachers began to creak as students gathered their bags.

"If you're interested in having a say in the future of your school, drop your name into the box by the gym doors," Mrs. Foose shouted. "I'll pick the names randomly, to keep it fair, and Principal Weeks will announce the board members tomorrow."

Brett hooked his backpack over his shoulder as he joined the surge of people pressing toward the double doors. "Are you gonna do it?" he asked, reaching for Frankie's hand. Her bolts buzzed with joy. Would she ever get tired of his chipped black nail polish and skull ring?

"Do what?" she asked.

"The Balance Board. Are you going to put your name in?"

Frankie giggled, appreciating his sense of humor almost as much as his willingness to accessorize. "It should be spelled like Balance B-O-R-E-D."

"I'm serious," he said. "You're always trying to get involved, so why not?"

"That was before," Frankie insisted, suddenly irritated. How many times did she have to remind him she was done with politics? She had fought and failed too many times. Besides, the fight was over. The RADs had won. It was time to partay! "If it's not fun, I'm done," she said. "I'm not wasting this weather sitting in after-school meetings."

"Looks like you're alone on that one," Brett said.

The sign-up box was surrounded by at least half the student body. All of the name cards had been used. A normie boy in a blue baseball hat wrote his info on a gum wrapper. Jackson Jekyll scribbled his on a yellow Post-it. Even Cleo was searching for something to write on.

"It's nice to see her getting involved," Frankie said, nodding toward Cleo. *Maybe now she'll be too busy to glare at me.*

"She's probably stuffing the ballot box so she can win," Billy said.

"What do you have against her?" Frankie asked. "She hasn't been mean to *you.*"

"I just don't want you to get hurt," Billy said with a hint of sarcasm. Frankie smiled. He was obviously making fun of her warnings about Spectra. But it was too sunny outside to care.

"Good luck," she said, smiling at Cleo as they walked out.

Cleo smirked. "Yeah, you too." Then she giggled.

Frankie considered telling Cleo she wasn't going to enter. But why bother? The sooner she got out of there, the faster she'd be hosting a pool party for her friends—which happened to be number seven on her to-do-or-die list. So she simply extended the invitation to Cleo and then bolted for the exit. One day closer to freedom!

17

CHAPTER TWO
VAMP OF APPROVAL

In the parking lot, winks of yellow sunlight glinted off the cars. Lala shaded her sensitive eyes as newly licensed drivers screeched into the first heat wave of summer. She shivered. Why couldn't the weather warm her the way Clawd Wolf did?

The Chic Freaks—Lala's proud nickname for Cleo, Frankie, Clawdeen, Blue, and herself—charged across the gum-spotted asphalt, not the least bit tempted by the end-of-day gossip or senior flirt sessions. Instead, their sunglass-covered eyes were fixed on Lala's Escalade. And she was running out of ways to stall them.

"Quit walking like a bludger!" Blue called over her shoulder. "My scales are crisping."

"My bolts are burning." (Frankie.)

"My fur is singeing." (Clawdeen.)

"Tan lines!" Cleo said, shielding her exposed shoulders under Clawdeen's thick auburn hair. "I need to get strapless before I turn all tic-tac-toe-y."

Lala slowed even more. "Do you need parasols?" she asked,

twirling the pink stem of the one in her hand. "I have a bunch in my locker. How 'bout I run back and—"

"Just put some go-go juice in your boots, will ya?" Clawdeen barked, doubling back to yank Lala forward. "Frankie's pool. Remember?"

Of course she remembered. They'd told her the instant they found her in the corner spooning with her space heater during the assembly. She wasn't stupid; she was in love. And leaving school without a kiss from Clawd felt like losing a purse and not being allowed to look for it. But try explaining that to his *I-still-can't-believe-you-think-he's-cute* sister.

Blue peeled back her sleeve and checked her pink G-Shock watch. "It hasn't rained in two hundred eleven hours. This town is as dry as the outback," she said. "If I get on the Balance Board, I'm gonna put pool lanes in the halls and swim to my classes."

Frankie whipped off her studded sunglasses. "You signed up for that?"

Cleo snickered, as if remembering a joke.

"So did I." Clawdeen lifted her auburn curls off her fur-lined neck and fanned. "If I get on, I'm hiring a groomer."

"I'm going to cover the walls with mirrors," Cleo announced.

"What do mirrors have to do with being a mummy?" Frankie asked.

"Nothing," Cleo replied with a smirk. "I just like looking at myself."

The Chic Freaks cracked up as they teetered in their platforms toward the Escalade. A mint-green Vespa zipped by, and Frankie blew a kiss in its direction.

"Want that!" she shouted over the buzzing motor. And then

she turned to Lala. "Looks like we're the only ones who didn't sign up for that board thingy."

Cleo giggled again.

"I signed up," Lala said, aware of how odd that remark must sound coming from her. She was hardly one to shy away from activism, but animal rescue and preservation had always been her thing, and that cause kept her busy outside of school. "Plenty of people are looking out for us, but who's looking out for them?" she liked to say when someone asked her to volunteer for something school-related. No one even bothered to ask anymore.

"I thought rescue-animal makeovers were your latest obsession," Clawdeen said.

"Yeah, what happened to beastiesB4besties?" Cleo teased, recalling Lala's old e-mail address.

"I did this for a beast," she explained. "Well, more like a bat."

"The old fella?" Blue asked, scratching her arms. Fine iridescent dust fell to the hot pavement.

Lala nodded, knowing Blue was referring to the big D, Lala's dad. "He thinks my leadership skills are suffering because I don't participate in school activities."

"Why does a pet aesthetician need leadership skills?" Frankie asked.

Lala lowered the pink ruffled parasol in front of her face. "He claims I won't get into a good college unless I prove my devotion to Merston."

"Got it!" Blue said, raising her finger. "How 'bout we find you a lovable little bluey and name him Merston?"

They burst out laughing again.

"What?" Clawdeen called, glancing back at the school. Across

20

the grassy lawn, out of earshot for non-canines, Clawd was saying something to her.

"What?" she asked again, this time in annoyance. Then, with a sigh, "Fine, but hurry up."

He fist-bumped his buddies and shuffled toward the parking lot with the enthusiasm of someone going to the principal's office. No waves, no smiles, no eye contact. No acknowledgment whatsoever that he even knew Lala. Clawd put the *cool* in *school*, at least when the boys were around. Still, her insides began to rev. Clawd always managed to kick up her cardio.

"What did he say?" Lala asked.

"Ask him," Clawdeen huffed. "He's coming to see you, not me."

"He said that?" Lala asked. "In front of the guys?"

" 'Course not," Clawdeen answered. "He said he had to get his football stuff from the car. But we know what that really means."

Yay!

Lala tossed her VEGAN PRINCESS key chain through the air to Clawdeen, who caught it like a bouquet. "Don't even think of turning on the AC," she shouted as the other girls ran for the Escalade.

Finally alone and leaning against the hood of Clawd's blue car, she grinned. *One kiss, coming right up!*

"Whaddaya think of my new heater?" Lala asked, patting the sun-warmed hood as he strolled toward her.

Clawd crinkled his thick brows as if offended. "Something wrong with the old one?"

"You're my *fur*nace," she said, ditching the car hood for the warmth of his chest.

As usual, he glanced over his shoulder to make sure no one was watching before he leaned in.

"Am I that embarrassing?" Lala asked, pulling away from his rough football jersey. She lifted her dark eyes to meet his. More yellow than Clawdeen's, they were like two burning embers.

" 'Course not," he said, running a hand over his green mohawk.

"Then why can't you treat me in public the way you do when we're alone?" she asked. "Melody Carver's into the Jekyll-and-Hyde thing, not me. It's time you let those guys know you care about more than throwing the chicken skin."

"Footballs are pigskin, not chicken skin."

"Could have fooled me, chicken," she teased. "Anyway, why are they made of skin at all? Aren't there any synthetic options?"

He lifted his hand and pressed it against her lips. "Stop. I have practice in three minutes. Do you want to talk about footballs?"

Lala poked him with her left fang. "No."

"Good. 'Cause I have something for you" he said, reaching into his backpack.

"What is it? You didn't need to get me anything...."

He pulled out a rectangle wrapped in aluminum foil.

Lala stepped back. "I'm not trying any more of your gross *Top Chef* experiments! That salty pudding thing was—"

He cut her off. "Just open it."

She pulled off the foil and uncovered a framed photo of Clawd in a navy wingback chair by a roaring fire. He was leaning intently over a chessboard, hands on his knees. A white queen hovered six inches above the board.

"That was nine months ago. At the Hideout Inn. Remember?" he asked bashfully.

"That was my winning move." Lala did a victorious booty roll. "I beat you like an egg."

"It was kind of like our first date," Clawd said, ignoring the dig. He had a hard enough time losing to a football team. "I know you don't show up in pictures, but I thought you might like it anyway. You can look at it during the full moon, when I'm not around."

Chirping birds flapped around the maples behind them. Lala rested her head against his chest, listening to the rapid beat of his heart. "It's fang-tastic."

He craned his neck as if working out a kink and mumbled, "You make me rabid happy."

Lala hugged the photo and then him. He grinned and lifted her chin just as the sounds of Rihanna began pumping from her Escalade. She kissed him anyway. Warm at last.

Honk! Honk!

"Let's go!" Clawdeen shouted, her head poking out the passenger side window.

"Heel!" Lala called.

Clawd popped open his trunk and traded out his backpack for a black Adidas gym bag. "It's okay. I've got practice anyway."

Lala smile-nodded. He quickly kissed her good-bye and then sprinted to the field.

"Who's ready to get 'On the Floor'?" Lala called as she hopped into the driver's seat and cranked J-Lo inside the SUV.

"Wooooo-hoooo!" they shouted from the open windows.

"Clawd's been so much cooler since you guys started hanging out," said Clawdeen.

Lala beamed. "How?"

Her friend smiled. "He's never around."

Laughter exploded from the backseat. In spite of the gusting air-conditioning, warmth enveloped Lala like a cashmere throw.

Just as she turned the Escalade onto Radcliffe Way, Lala's iPhone chimed its weekly reminder.

"Hold on tight!" she called, and then stomped on the gas pedal. Clawdeen slammed into Cleo's seat. Blue fell into the center console, and Frankie's green legs flew up, flashing the girls a glimpse of her striped boyshorts.

Lala screeched to a stop under the canopy of wide-leafed maples in front of her house and hopped out to hurry toward the Victorian mansion, not needing to explain her abrupt exit. It was Wednesday at three forty-five, and her phone had sounded the alert. Her friends knew exactly where she was going.

The hallway—velvet-covered walls and black marble floors lit by dim puddles of light—left visitors temporarily blind. But Lala's eyes adjusted instantly as the smell of burning firewood welcomed her home.

A familiar *pata-pat-pat-pata-pat-pat* sound, like a mouse scurrying in tap shoes, grew louder. And then, "*Eeeeeeeeeeeeeee eeeeeeeeeeee.*"

"Count Fabulous!" Lala cooed, making a perch of her arm. The fist-sized bat relaxed his wings and glided to a stop on her stack of bracelets. He was still wearing the pink bow she'd tied behind his ears earlier that day. But he'd managed to flap off most of the gold wing dust. Typical male.

"I know you're hungry, but Daddy's waiting," Lala told her pet.

"*Eeeeeeeeeeeeeeeeeeeeeeeeeeee,*" he screeched, flapping back up the stairs toward their bedroom. Nine years old and he was still terrified of Mr. D.

Lala tossed her fuchsia microfiber tote onto a black-and-gold velvet bench and then hurried down the hallway that was lined with generations of vampire portraits modernized by high-gloss lacquer frames. The corridor looked more like the celebrity-studded walls of Sardi's restaurant in New York than a tribute to an ancient bloodline. But there was nothing ancient about Mr. D. He liked his home the way Lala liked her hair: sleek, dark, and luxurious.

She followed the sound of her uncle's raspy voice to the parlor—which was an homage to Armani's decadent home-furnishing line. Instead of historical relics or valuable works of art, a sixty-four-inch flat screen was mounted to crinkled-for-effect gold wallpaper.

Standing before it was Uncle Vlad, a small man with tousled gray hair and round tortoiseshell glasses. With his arms crossed over his double-breasted blue cardigan, he looked like a fed-up gnome.

"I know you called to speak to Lala," Uncle Vlad said. "But first you and I need to talk color scheme. The fang shui in here is totally off. We need a dash of happy." He gestured to the glass hearth around the fireplace, the black daybed, the black shag rug, the black lacquer console with pleated doors. "I feel like I'm trapped inside a violin case."

Lala giggled.

"We've been over this," Mr. D's deep voice bellowed from the screen. "I refuse to believe bright colors and the location of furniture can solve problems. If you want good things, you have to go out into the world and *get* them. Now, where's my daughter?"

Lala zipped into the frame. "Here, Daddy."

Uncle Vlad stepped aside, dabbing his slick forehead with a pale pink kerchief. A slow eye roll let Lala know that stalling for her was stressing him out big-time.

She bit her bottom lip. *Sorry!*

Uncle Vlad stuffed his small hands in the pockets of his plaid pants and hurried toward the pantry to eat his emotions.

"Hey, Dad," Lala said, sitting stiffly on the edge of the daybed.

On-screen, the deeply tanned man with slicked-back hair nodded once. He was wearing a sharply creased silver-gray suit and sat behind a polished wood desk with a row of round windows behind him. Glimpses of bright blue sky and turquoise sea bobbed in and out of view. His black eyes were stern as he examined his daughter's outfit.

Lala crossed her pink-stockinged legs and leaned forward, doing what she could to conceal the frilly black miniskirt he had once said would get her the kind of attention she wanted but not the kind she needed. Lala pulled a wool throw over her tight black blazer. Even with the fire roaring and the central heat kicked up to Bahamas, she began to shiver. Blood and warmth: Her father had a knack for sucking them both.

"So." Mr. D's voice was clipped and hurried. "Any news?"

Lala looked up. For the first time, she did have something to report.

"Um, look what I got," she said, holding up the picture of Clawd.

Mr. D lightly steepled his fingertips and then pressed them to his lips.

"It's Clawd. My boyfriend. Clawdeen's brother?"

He narrowed his eyes. "A Wolf?"

Lala nodded slowly.

"Anything else?" he managed. "Anything you can be proud of? Anything that might further your personal growth as a leader?"

Ashamed, Lala lowered her gaze to the black ribbon laces on

her boots. She considered telling him she had applied for the Balance Board. But what if she wasn't chosen? He'd be even more disappointed.

"I got an A on my biology quiz," she lied.

He tried to smile. It looked like gut pain. "Did you sign up for that summer school teacher's aide program?"

"It's full," she lied again.

Mr. D sighed. "Of course it is."

Sorry, Dad, okay? I'm not class president, and I don't want to be. I'm not obsessed with college applications or leadership skills or power. My friends and family aren't afraid of me, and I don't want them to be. Animals don't hide when they hear me coming. And everyone thinks my outfits are fang-tastic. Maybe if you moved back here instead of living on that yacht, you'd see that. And then you'd love me the way I am. Because I love you the way you are, Lala wanted to shout. Instead, she promised she'd find another college-application-worthy pastime the minute they hung up.

Lala faced the empty screen. Now what? It was June. Opportunities to "better" Merston High were hardly flooding her in-box. But if she wanted her father's approval, she'd have to do something. Take initiative. Try.

She hurried over to the laptop blinking on an antique mirrored credenza and Googled OPPORTUNITY HELP SCHOOL. About 730,000,000 results popped up. Lala began scrolling and stopped at number thirteen.

And there it was. The high school extracurricular dream. Whoever had said that number was unlucky was about to be proved wrong. Dead wrong.

27

CHAPTER THREE
SUBSTITUTE CREATURE

A swarm of stylishly disheveled hipsters inched toward the squat brick building, drawn to the yellow light spilling from the open door.

Despite the warm night, Melody Carver zipped her black hoodie and folded her arms across her chest. Was she seriously outside a college pub dressed in a bleach-stained Hello Kitty tee, striped pajamas, and UGG flip-flops? She was the one with the influential Siren voice. She was supposed to be telling other people what to do. And yet somehow her older sister, Candace, a normie, had her beat when it came to persuasion.

"IDs," grumbled the thick-necked bouncer. He wielded his black penlight Darth Vader–style.

A doe-eyed pixie at the front of the line stepped forward, flashing her card and an eye roll. "I'm here, like, every night," she told her friends. "Does he seriously need to check?"

"When you grow to five-nine and weigh a hundred and fifty-five pounds, I'll stop. Now beat it, Bambi," he said, waving the next person forward.

"Nice pit stains!" the petite girl shouted, wobble-stomping away in wedges as high as the box they came in.

"Next!"

A boy in skinny jeans patted his pockets frantically as a guy in a white muscle tee and tattoo sleeves fist-bumped Pit Stains and cruised inside.

"Clear your throat," Candace mumbled from the side of her poppy-red mouth. "We're next."

They inched forward. The humid air smelled like cigarettes and patchouli oil. Fearing an asthma attack, Melody waved away the smoke. Candace smacked her. "Stop acting high school."

"But I'm *in* high—"

"Tonight you're not!" Candace fluffed her blond curls.

"I can't believe Shane hasn't busted you yet." Melody giggled, amazed. "Does he honestly think you go to Willamette College?"

"Why wouldn't he?"

"For one thing, he never sees you on campus," Melody said, suddenly needing to pee. Why had she drunk that thirty-two-ounce Dr Pepper? Oh yeah, because she'd thought she would be at home studying for her math test, not working a dive-bar bouncer so Candace could meet her college boyfriend.

Candace plucked an olive-colored feather from Melody's hair and tucked it behind her own ear. "Accessorizing is so easy when you're around. I swear, everyone should have a Siren for a sister."

"I think someone should have *you* for a sister," Melody teased. "I need a break."

Behind them, a brunette wearing a flannel dress and combat boots was examining Candace. Melody was used to it by now. Her sister's beachy good looks and city style were checked out more than the library's copy of *Twilight*.

A girl with dreadlocks tapped Candace on her shimmer-dusted shoulder. "Hey, Barbie. Like, prom is next month."

"'Scuse me?" Candace asked, confused.

Melody's heart thumped. It always did when she was about to get bullied. What would it be tonight? Her slippers? Her pajamas? Her tangled hair?

"You think you're gonna get past Mini dressed like that?" asked Flannel.

"She belongs on top of a birthday cake." (Dreads.)

"Or a parade float." (Flannel.)

"Or a hill of Skittles." (Dreads.)

Flannel burst out laughing. "What's a hill of Skittles?"

Dreads blew a line of smoke from her thin lips and shrugged. "I have no idea."

They laughed together.

Shock overshadowed Melody's urge to pee. These girls were making fun of her sister's clothes, not hers. For once!

Candace stepped into Dread's personal space. She put her hands on her hips and—

"Next!" called Mini.

Melody pulled Candace forward.

Rattled by her first experience with criticism, Candace was stunned into silence. "Um…"

Flannel leaned forward and muttered, "At least I look over twenty-one."

Candace's green eyes snapped back to life. "At least I don't!" She pulled a business card out of her beaded clutch and flicked it toward the other girl. "Don't worry. My dad's a plastic surgeon. If you ever win the lottery, call him. He loves a challenge."

Melody couldn't help laughing at the girls' shocked faces. Trust Candace to have the perfect comeback.

"I said, IDs!"

Candace shoved Melody forward.

Please let my voice work, please let my voice work. Excluding the call she had made to the University of Southern California's admissions office (Candace had needed more time on her entrance essay, and Melody had needed Candace to stop begging her for help), Melody hadn't used her Siren skills in months. Controlling destiny was too much responsibility for her. She'd learned her lesson after Clawdeen's Sassy Sixteen. And again when she got the server at Dairy Queen to load Jackson's Blizzard with every mix-in on the menu. That night he had puked gummy bear/Oreo/ graham cracker all over her new jean jacket.

Melody took a deep breath and looked directly into Mini's black eyes. "You do not need to see our IDs. We are twenty-one. The two girls behind us are not."

He began blinking. It was working.

He placed a warm hand on Melody's back and ushered her and Candace into the yellow light.

Candace slipped her arm through Melody's and squeezed. "I told you it would be fine!"

The pee pain returned, but Melody smiled anyway. Not so much because she got in. But because for once, she didn't stand out.

The musty air smelled like beer and stale popcorn. Melody desperately scanned the crowded venue for a bathroom while her eyes adjusted to the dim light.

A scarred wooden bar ran the length of the room. Behind it an Asian hipster in a black tee and Dickies tended to the three-deep crowd. Tall tables were like gigantic coasters for empty pints and purses, and college students mingled and bobbed to the Cure track that was blasting from the speakers by the stage. The music was a placeholder, a distraction while the all-girl band set up.

Melody thought back to her days as a singer, before the asthma. Performances were for grown-ups seated in auditoriums and smelling like expensive perfumes. She tried to imagine singing for people her own age. The idea quickly became a feeling; it was a lot like falling.

"I'm off to find Shane. You sure you're okay getting home?" Candace asked, smudging her eyeliner to look like a sexy accident.

Melody had gotten her license only six days before, but she was consumed with not peeing her pajama pants, so she nodded convincingly. Candace tossed her the keys and then bolted.

Finally.

The narrow black bathroom was plastered with posters and stickers from some of her favorite bands: Foo Fighters, Pearl Jam, Nirvana, Blind Melon, STP.... It was like an homage to nineties grunge. Or rather an homage to the dark music she had played in sunny Beverly Hills. Songs for outcasts. Songs for her.

Washing her hands with cold water and no soap in the wobbly

pedestal sink, Melody checked her reflection in the cracked mirror. She certainly didn't look her best. Tangled black hair tied in a messy ponytail, scattered feathers dangling by the sides of her face, narrow gray eyes propped open by caffeine. She was no Candace, that's for sure. But tonight that didn't seem to matter. No one seemed to notice Melody. It was incredible.

As she pushed her way toward the exit, the lights dimmed. The crowd gathered in front of the stage and began cheering.

A blond in tight cutoffs and a half shirt that exposed a roll of belly fat that didn't seem to faze her took a seat behind a worn drum kit mended with duct tape. A girl with pink hair, a silver bra, and black skinny jeans plugged her bass into an old amp with a peeling sticker that said BAD CAT. The guitar player wore a poofy blue prom dress, torn fishnets, and combat boots. Once they were situated, a brunette with a high-gloss ponytail and an off-the-shoulder black jersey tee stomped onto the stage. Her white leather booties reflected the dirty wood floor. She looked more like an indignant cheerleader than a fellow rocker.

"Heyyyy, boozers and losers!" she called. "My name is Davina, and I'm about to rock your cock-a-doodle-doos!"

Her bandmates exchanged an irritated glance. Pink Hair leaned into her mike and added, "And we're Grunge Goddess."

Everyone cheered.

"Oops, forgot about them." Davina girlie-giggled. "My rude."

"We're used to it," shouted the drummer, knocking her sticks together. "Five, six, sev-uhn, eight!"

Which reminded Melody—math test! It was time to go. And

33

then familiar chords blasted through the bar. Pearl Jam? She couldn't leave now.

Melody began shoving her way toward the stage.

"Watch it!" called a blue-haired girl in jeggings and a mesh tank top. Then Melody collided with a muscular mass in a dark gray tee.

"You okay?" he asked, gripping her shoulder. Despite the cluster of sweaty bodies, his hand was surprisingly cool. She nodded and slipped past him.

"Follow us," said a familiar boy's voice. It was Billy and his violet-scented girlfriend, Spectra: Merston High's beloved invisible couple. They pulled her to the front of the stage with dexterity. They had navigated these crowds before.

As the spotlight roamed, Melody caught a glimpse of Spectra. The light moved on, and the purple-haired ethereal beauty in a black tank dress disappeared. "What are you doing here?" Melody asked.

"I've been coming here for years. The music is awesome."

Melody nodded her head vigorously and flashed Spectra two geeky thumbs up. Then she held her arms up and cheered as the band played "State of Love and Trust."

"Where's your sister?" Billy asked.

"Shane," Melody called.

"Look who I met!" shouted Candace, dancing toward them in the center of a three-person conga line. "Rudy and Byron."

"Brian," said the guy in the front.

"Then stop saying your name is Byron," Candace said.

"I didn't!"

Candace jumped out of the line. "I don't conga with liars."

For the next thirty minutes, they danced and laughed through the best of the nineties. Melody's math book beckoned, but each song was better than the last. She couldn't pull away from the thumping bass notes and the moaning guitar. From the music that had been her friend when no one else was interested.

Onstage, Davina half-swallowed the microphone and swung her ponytail like a revving chopper. She turned her back to the crowd and slapped her Pilates-toned butt.

The song began to build, and Melody sang along. Bouncing up and down as the chorus peaked, she surrendered to the collective energy of the crowd. Chugging Red Bull while getting shot from a cannon probably felt like this.

A sudden longing for Jackson gripped Melody like a zipped leather jacket. She wanted him there. Needed him to know this part of her. Music roused something inside her the way Jackson's sweat roused D.J. She had witnessed his transformation, and she wanted him to see hers. Life's special moments didn't feel real anymore unless they were shared. That was love. But wasn't love also leaving him alone so he could study for their math test?

Davina was at the front of the stage, leaning toward the audience. "Catch me, you chapped-lipped weaklings!" she shouted. And then—arms splayed, chin up, toes together—she dove. She glided through the air toward her fans with the assurance of a wide-winged seabird. "Incominggggg!"

Bodies scattered like roaches from Raid.

Thump. Awreeeeeeeeeeee. The fallen microphone shot feedback through the bar as it—and Davina—crash-landed on the sticky floor with an amplified *ooof.*

Audience members searched the club frantically, as if expecting a friend who still hadn't shown. The band continued to play.

"My shoulder!" cried Davina. "I think I broke something...."

The bouncer appeared and knelt in front of the injured diva. He picked her up like a baby bird and slung her injured wing around his neck.

She kicked him in the shin. "Oww!" she snapped. "That's the broken one!"

"Ooops." He winked at the band as he hauled her off. "My rude."

The girls onstage suppressed their smiles.

"Aren't they worried about her?" Melody asked.

"They hate Davina," Spectra explained. "She's such a snob. She doesn't even know these songs—they have to bribe her with clothes or she won't practice."

"Why didn't they kick her out?" Melody asked.

"Her father is Danny Corrigan," Billy explained, tilting her head to face the neon sign above the bar. "As in Corrigan's. It's his place. And right now this is the only place they play."

"I heard that Sage, the guitarist, paid the people in the front row to drop Davina!" Spectra said, with the certainty of someone who could back up her statement with proof, even though she rarely did.

"Anyone know 'Doll Parts'?" Sage asked, swaying in her combats.

Melody gasped. She'd been singing that song in the shower for, like, forever. She could sing it backward while chewing gum. But there was no way she could get up in front of a crowd like this. What if her asthma kicked in? What if ...

"She does!" Candace called, lifting her sister's hand in the air.

Melody ducked. But Billy wrapped his arms around her knees and lifted her up.

"Her name is Melly!" Candace shouted. A wavy-haired guy with wire-framed glasses and a face full of study-stubble appeared at her side. Candace hugged him like a returning war hero. *Shane?*

"She's coming!" Spectra yelled.

"Melly! Melly! Melly!" chanted Spectra and Billy. Seconds later everyone else joined in.

"Melly! Melly! Melly!"

Melody stiffened. She was going to kill Candace…if she herself didn't die of embarrassment first.

Candace grabbed Melody by the shoulders. Her green eyes were sincere. Loving, even. "You know what Mom always says? What would you do if you knew you couldn't fail?" Melody clenched her fists as if knowing the answer and refusing to let it go. Candace winked. "Fear out!"

With the help of Billy, Spectra, and Shane, Candace pushed her sister forward. Sage extended a calloused hand to pull Melody up onto the stage.

"Nice pj's." The guitarist grinned, meaning it. "From the beginning?" she whispered, and then tossed Melody the mike.

Melody swallowed the Dr Pepper–flavored barf rising in her throat. Faces glared up at her. If only one of them had belonged to Jackson. They didn't have the warm, loving expressions he would have. Instead, they seemed impatient, restless, and ready to revolt. Their skepticism rose over the strumming guitar, dismissing her as an amateur before she even started.

Melody closed her eyes. She could do this. She had done this.

37

She had always dreamed of doing it again. All she had to do was ignore the talking, shut out their doubtful expressions, step back into the shower, and...

"I am doll eyes..."

Her voice was clean. No wheezing. No phlegm. Just pure and haunting.

Suddenly, Melody was back in Beverly Hills. Angry at the world for dismissing her because of a (massive) nose. Reduced to a body part instead of seen as a whole person. Raging in the shower while her family was out and about, enjoying their beauty.

Sage's guitar was insistent. Melody gripped the microphone with both hands, embodying the energy of drums, the bass. Her indignation grew, gathering force like a spiraling tornado.

"Yeah, they really want you, they really want you, they really do..."

The music began to slow. The song was winding down. She adjusted her voice accordingly. From anger to vengeance to vulnerability to surrender.

"Someday, you will ache like I ache..."

With a final strum, the song ended. The room was silent. Melody opened her eyes.

Applause popped like a piñata.

She smiled humbly.

"Know any Nirvana?" Sage asked.

Melody nodded.

CHAPTER FOUR
LOOK WHAT THE BAT DRAGGED IN

Count Fabulous swooped down from the top of Lala's black canopied coffin bed. Claws extended, he gnashed his tiny yellow teeth and headed straight for—

"Stop! It's not a real mouse!" She caught her leathery pet before he touched down on her keypad and messed up her document. As she scratched his downy head, a string of bat drool dropped onto her pink silk pajamas.

"Ewwww!" Irish Emmy scampered off the ruffled throw pillows and smashed into the silver handles that lowered the top of Lala's custom coffin bed. The hardening clay mask on her face fissured.

"Everyone drools in America, Emmy," Blue joked, polishing a caramel-colored poodle's toenails. "Look at Teeny Turner." The aforementioned maltipoo pup, who smacked of the singer when her curls were combed out, was snoring peacefully. Beneath her muzzle a wet spot slowly spread across the black satin chaise.

Irish Emmy looked around at the fidgety rescue pets in stacked wire cages and dog crates lined with yellow-stained newspaper. "I know. It just feels like I'm a chiseler again back on the farm."

"No need to grizzle, Sheila," Blue said. "You're behind the scenes of a ridgy-didgy rescue-animal fashion show. Ain't nothing farmy about it."

"Fur real," Clawdeen added. "I thought you wanted to help us," she said, referring to her video blog, Where There's a Wolf, There's a Way. They were about to film her DIY line of animal accessories, and Irish Emmy had volunteered to work the camera.

"Cheers, I do," insisted Irish Emmy as she fanned the air with a quesadilla.

Lala wanted to tell her friends to keep it down. Between their endless unintelligible chatter and Blue's bonzer playlist 7.0, it was impossible to concentrate. But the letter she was writing should have been done by now. What was supposed to take hours had taken days.

"Can't we open a window?" Clawdeen asked, looking at the assortment of screened and tinted windows near the vaulted ceiling. "Teeny Turner's paw-dicure will never dry in this humidity." Her luxurious auburn fur was jeweled with droplets of mist from the frog-shaped humidifier that breathed steam over the terrarium for Kale and Sprout, two turtles with denim pockets glued to their shells.

"Kale has a cough," Lala said. "The cold air is bad for him." *And me!*

"Well, something's gotta give," Irish Emmy said. "The reek is right brutal in here."

Lala turned away from her computer with a frustrated sigh. "Count Fabulous, open the top, please."

The bat flew up to the ceiling and began poking his head against the pink-and-black-striped wallpaper. One by one, heart-shaped holes appeared. Beams of moonlight seeped in, and the stale air drained out.

"Cheers!" Irish Emmy clapped. "I'm feelin' like a critter in a shoe box on show-'n'-tell day."

"Clawd made them for me after a crow flew in the regular window and snatched Snake Gyllenhaal from his cage," Lala said.

Irish Emmy pouted as though that was the most adorable thing she'd ever heard.

Someone knocked. Teeny Turner jumped off the bed and ran toward the door. Small beaded braids on her soft woolly ears bounced and clacked.

"Come in," Lala called.

Uncle Vlad balanced on one foot and used the other to nudge open the door. The dog pounced and scratched at the toe of Vlad's custom-designed purple-and-red-checked Vans. "Down, Mariah—or whatever your name is.... Make like Michael Jackson and beat it!" Dressed in bright plaid shorts and a turquoise Hollister sweater, he balanced a precarious stack of steaming quesadillas on a gold tray as if he were some kind of circus clown. Soda cans began to wobble. Blue jumped up to take the tray.

"Wow, I haven't seen so much glitter since my Studio 54 days," Vlad said, taking in his surroundings.

"Thanks." Clawdeen smiled proudly.

Vlad strutted toward the computer to the beat of Katy Perry's "California Gurls." He leaned over Lala's shoulder and tsked at the computer screen.

"I know, I know. But it's only..." She peered up at the sky and

41

evaluated the position of the moon. "Seven forty-five." She glanced at Clawdeen, who confirmed with a nod. "I still have fifteen minutes."

"C'mon, Sheila, give us a peek," Blue said, patting Kitson, an orange kitten with a belly chain and magnetic clip-on hoops (engineered for sensitive feline ears).

"Yeah, make like BP oil and spill," Uncle Vlad said.

Lala spun slowly in her chair, wishing she were alone with the animals, as she usually was. Dozens of moist eyes watched her lovingly, without judgment. Her animals didn't give a hoot, a bark, or a squeak about college applications or leadership skills. They were grateful just because she cared. They never wanted to leave on business trips or cut phone calls short because they were late for a meeting. They were more humane than most humans.

"Hurry up," Clawdeen urged, anxious to start filming her video blog.

Lala took a deep breath. If she had a beating heart, it would be racing. Where to begin? She considered taking them back to the phone call she had with her dad, and her online search for an extracurricular activity, but her deadline was approaching, so she went for the bottom-line version. "Brigitte T'eau Shoes and Dally Sports Apparel have merged—"

"Pause!" Vlad lifted his palm like a crossing guard. "It's not pronounced *Two*; it's pronounced *Toe*." He took off his tortoise-shell glasses and rubbed the bridge of his nose like someone who couldn't take it anymore. "If that mademoiselle heard you butcher her last name like pâté, you would be dead meat."

The girls giggled.

"Sorry," Lala said. "So...the French designer Brigitte *Toe* and Dally Sports Apparel merged to create a shoe that brings together fashion and function. It's called the T'eau Dally."

Uncle Vlad clapped. "*J'adore!* What's next? Jimmy Choo and Reebok? They could call it ChooBok-a."

Everyone laughed but Lala. She was too stressed for jokes. "Anyway, they're holding a contest to find a school that brings together different kinds of people, the way they did with their shoes. And Merston would be perfect."

Emmy cracked open an icy soda. "What's the prize?"

"The winner becomes the first sponsored school in America." Lala spun faster in her chair. "And gets a million dollars to upgrade."

"More pools!" (Blue.)

"A grooming kiosk!" (Clawdeen.)

"Bang-on cafeteria food that doesn't taste like donkey arse!" (Irish Emmy.)

"Wallpaper!" Uncle Vlad chimed in.

"And central heat," Lala added. "Plus, they want a couple from the school to star in their national ad campaign."

"You and Clawd would be ace!" Blue said, leaning against the foot of the coffin bed. The Worminator, a trembling yellow budgie, stuck his nose out from under the bed and pecked the carpet for errant seeds. Blue pinched some orange cheese off her quesadilla and waved it in front of his beak.

"Stop!" Lala shouted, grabbing the cheese. "He's lactose-intolerant. Try the escarole."

Uncle Vlad gestured toward the untouched crudités platter he'd dropped off earlier. "Glad someone's enjoying it," he mumbled.

43

"What about a new arts-and-crafts studio? With sewing machines and jewelry making..." Clawdeen was using purple and black nontoxic mascaras to paint hearts on a white bunny.

A bat-cave-sized pit opened in Lala's stomach. *Wait!* she wanted to scream. *I have to win first!* She twirled a piece of hair around her left fang as if she were five again.

Vlad put his icy hand on her shoulder.

She forced herself to breathe slowly. *In through the nose, out through the mouth...* Her dark eyes scanned the words on her computer screen. The thing with writing was that it was never done. Sentences could always be better. Words more lyrical. Grammar more good.

Blue fed another bite of escarole to the Worminator. "Let's have a Captain Cook. We'll tell ya if its bodgy."

"Yeah, hurry up and read it to us," Clawdeen said, smoothing the miniature orange-and-fuchsia sequined tulle skirt she'd made for Fuego's sister, Caliente.

Lala turned down the music and cleared her throat. "Don't laugh, okay?"

"Game up and read it already, will ya?" Irish Emmy said.

Lala sighed. "Okay, here goes...." She began to read the message aloud.

Dear Brigitte T'eau Shoes and Dally Sports Apparel,

My name is Lala. Short for Draculaura. I'm a huge fan of T'eau footwear, and I'm sure I would love Dally sportswear, only I'm not superathletic. My boyfriend, Clawd, is on the football team, though. And he has four pairs. Three with those spiky things on the bottom so he doesn't slip, and a pair of cross-trainers for full-moon nights, when he has to run through the woods and hide so he doesn't freak out the normies.

Anyway, we go to Merston High. You know, that school in Salem, Oregon, that's been in the news lately because we have monsters? Just in case Ms. T'eau hasn't heard of us (not because she's clueless but because she lives in France, and I assume that country has its own news). I know we'd be perfect for your merger contest.

For example, I'm a vampire. (Don't worry, you're safe with me. Blood makes me faint. True story!) And my boyfriend is a werewolf. So is my best friend, Clawdeen. We are also friends with mummies, Franken-stein's granddaughter, invisibles, sea monsters, a Siren, zombies, a split personality, a Gorgon, and a ton of normies (people like you, unless you're hiding something, LOL).

We in the Regular Attribute Dodger (or RAD) community used to live in total hiding. But over the past six months, we have come out of the shoe closet (get it?) and merged with the normies at our school. We are just like your shoes, only alive—well, most of us anyway.☺

We would love to be the first sponsored high school in North America. We would put your logo on everything. Your sponsorship would really help us upgrade our school to accommodate the different needs of the RADs and would give others the courage to live openly. Oh, and I would be a fang-tastic leader.

Lala

P.S. I have the T'eau Mary Janes, in oxblood, from 2009. You really should consider bringing them back. The strap tore off my left one, and I'm dying for another pair. (Not literally. I can't really die. Not anymore, at least. Which is another reason I'd make a great leader.)

45

"Brava!" Vlad dabbed his eyes with his ascot.

"Deadly fierce!" Irish Emmy cheered.

"Mad corker!" Blue shouted.

Clawdeen clapped her hands. "Perfect!" Lala wasn't sure if Clawdeen was clapping because the letter was good or just because now they could focus on her video blog. "I knew it would be great, La! Send it."

Lala read through the letter one more time. Her lips moved silently as her dark eyes tracked across the glowing screen. She glanced at Vlad. He winked. She sighed and kissed her fingertips, pressing them to the screen. "Okay, here goes..." *This is for you, Dad.* She hit Send and instantly felt like she could breathe again. *You can't say I didn't try.* Then she jumped up and grabbed some ribbons. "You guys start on the intro while Blue, Vlad, and I put the final touches on the models."

Irish Emmy switched on her video camera and started pressing buttons on the side.

Clawdeen pulled out a compact and fluffed up her curls. She checked her teeth for berry-colored lip stain and then tossed the mirror into her red bag. Standing in front of the camera, she put a hand on her hip. "How do I look?"

Irish Emmy peered through the viewfinder. "Cracker. All we need'r lights."

"Roger Dodger." Blue adjusted a chrome task lamp and pointed the 150-watt bulb directly at Clawdeen's face. Lala and Vlad squinted.

"Clawdeen in three...two..." Irish Emmy held up a single finger and then pointed at the host.

"Welcome to another episode of Where There's a Wolf, There's a Way. I'm Clawdeen Wolf and—" Teeny Turner barked.

"Still rolling," Irish Emmy said. "I can edit that on my lappy. Carry on."

Clawdeen stopped abruptly and froze, as if listening to a far-off sound.

Irish Emmy kept her camera cocked. "Keep firing away, lass."

Clawdeen shook her head. "Sorry. I thought I heard—"

The desk lamp flickered.

Blue held Kale in her left hand and a paintbrush in her right. "What's going on?" she asked as the turtle's head drew back into his shell.

Squeaks came from a wire cage. Rat-a-tat screeched mournfully, his midnight-blue tail batting against the bars.

Clawdeen continued. "Teeny Turner was discovered wandering a road in Salem, Oregon. Her coat was dull and her claws were jagged until—"

"*Cut!*" Irish Emmy's head popped up. "Lala, can you do something about that noise?" The animals were starting to mewl, whine, growl, and hiss.

Lala raced to soothe her cagey pets.

"Cheers. Okay, rolling in three…two…" The room went coffin-dark. Irish Emmy's scream chilled the humid air. The desk lamp flickered. Clawdeen and Blue giggled nervously.

"Phooey on your energy-saving bulbs, Lala," Vlad huffed. "They save energy because they're never on."

"It's not the bulbs," Lala mumbled, wondering whether the

power was out in the T'eau Dally offices too. As long as her letter made it before the deadline—

The lights flashed back on.

"Right, then." Irish Emmy's voice was unsteady. "Still rolling."

Clawdeen stood uncertainly in front of the camera, took a deep breath, and continued. "Tonight, Teeny Turner is wearing L'Oreal's all-natural hair dye in russet red. An orange knit scarf, the same color as her paw polish and—"

Teeny whined and then shook off the scarf. It trailed behind her like toilet paper on a shoe as she squeezed under the bed.

Another thunder boom rolled across the house.

"Try the turtles," Lala whispered.

Clawdeen faced the camera. "These red-eared turtles were left in an Oregon pond to freeze by someone who didn't want to take care of them any longer...." Her voice was trembling.

"Ouch!" Blue dropped Kale back in his terrarium, where he promptly crawled into a plastic hollow log. "He bit me!"

"What's going on?" Lala asked no one in particular. "They've never freaked out like this before."

Teeny yelped from under the bed.

Clawdeen's ears tensed. "Lala," she began. "I think—"

"Daaaaad-dy's home," Vlad said.

CHAPTER FIVE
SPREE AT LAST!

The energy in the courtyard of the Salem Hills shopping center was electrifying. Frankie wanted to run through the pretzel-scented air screaming about the joy of living freely. She wanted to booty roll in the window of Forever 21—right between the green ribbed tank dress and the studded black mini—and show the passing shoppers her Lady Gaga "Star-struck" routine. She wanted the kids eating soft-serve on the fountain stairs and the lab-coated aestheticians straw-sucking Diet Cokes on their breaks to join in. She wanted to lead a flash mob of liberated dancers *Glee*-style.

Instead, she was strolling hand in hand with Brett past the three-tiered fountain, eating a passion fruit Pinkberry. Which was perfectly voltage; it just didn't require much energy, and Frankie had kilowatts to burn.

Maybe it was just the eighty-five-degree sun warming her shoulders. Or the leisurely way Brett's ripped jeans crinkled as he strolled, as if he had nowhere else to be but exactly where he was.

It could have been the window displays popping with bright summer separates like an all-you-can-afford buffet. But it was probably just the continued thrill of being in public in her birthday skin, without that pore-clogging makeup she used to wear. No bolt-hiding turtlenecks. No fear. Even though it was her twenty-seventh trip to this particular mall since she came out of hiding, it still felt too mint to be true.

A couple of college girls sharing an extra-large fro-yo dripping Cocoa Puffs and gummy bears smile-nodded as Frankie passed.

"Cute shoes," one of them said.

"Thanks!" Beaming, Frankie grinned down at her cork wedges. She always got compliments when she wore them with her periwinkle floral romper. They made her legs look extra long.

"How crazy is that?" Brett tossed the waxed paper from his pretzel into the trash.

"Why? My shoes are cute."

Brett snickered. "No. It's crazy that people don't even notice the color of your skin anymore. They just see...you."

Just then a boy with a pierced nose and tattoo sleeves whizzed by on his skateboard. He turned and glanced back at Frankie.

"Spoke too soon." She giggled. "I think he's a little freaked," she said, stopping to check the silver peep-toe combat boots in the window of the Steve Madden store.

Brett put his arm around her and pulled her close. "Ummm... I think he just thinks you're hot." He squeezed tighter, as if claiming her for himself. Just in case there was ever any doubt. Which there wasn't.

She squeezed him back. "Awwww...that is so sweet!" He leaned in and kissed her.

Frankie sparked until the moment he pulled away. The skateboarder had been staring. Frankie tried to console him with her friendliest wave, but he rolled away disappointed. *Did he really just see me for me?* Had they come that far? Was it—?

"Look!" she said, yanking Brett toward a pink-and-black awning. "There's a sale at Betsey Johnson!"

"What's up, Franks?" asked a glam-goth salesgirl. Her black-lined lips lifted in a welcoming smile.

"Just browsing."

"Ten percent off on anything in the store," the goth offered, tugging on her black lace scarf—one of six dangling around her neck.

"You having a sale?" Brett asked, obviously trying to show he could hold his own in a shopping situation.

"It's a Stein special."

"Awwwww." Frankie hugged her. She smelled like cherry perfume.

"You're a celebrity here," he said, as they wandered toward the accessories rack. Bolt earrings and leather cuffs with stitches sewn in were available in an array of unapologetic colors.

"It's not just me," she said, trying on an auburn faux-fur hair band. "It's all the RADs."

Outside, a crowd was gathering around a street performer. A mime was sweating off his makeup as he tossed three oranges in the air. Frankie pulled Brett toward the spectacle.

But Brett stopped under a shorn fig tree, desperate to keep his distance.

"What's wrong?" she asked, hating to miss a second of the show.

He pointed to his T-shirt: It was emblazoned with a cartoon of

51

a mime tied to a train track and inches away from being crushed by a speeding locomotive.

"That's not him, is it?"

Brett laughed. "No, but—"

Frankie stood on her tippy-toes, gave him a quick kiss, and dragged him toward the front of the crowd. The instant the mime saw Brett's shirt, he made a show of wiping invisible tears from his eyes and then ran off.

"Told ya," Brett said as he and Frankie burst into hysterics and took cover behind a bronze dolphin.

She pressed her cheek into his muscular chest. "Summer is going to be so voltage," she said, looking in the window of Nike. He smoothed her black hair off her forehead and tucked it behind her ears. "I was thinking we could take up tennis," she said.

Jutting his chin forward like a rich upper-cruster, he said, "Oh, Fritzy, I was just thinking the same thing. Your club or mine?"

Frankie giggled. "I'm serious."

"Why?"

"Name one sport that has cuter outfits," she said, imagining herself in the yellow pleated mini and matching sports bra in the store display.

"Skinny-dipping?" he tried.

She smacked him on the arm.

Holding hands, they strolled past a cart with canvas totes and stickers and posters imploring them to protect Mother Earth. Frankie picked up a button that said LOL LIVE OUT LOUD.

"I can't believe Saturday's almost over," she whined. Monday meant school. And school meant dealing with Cleo and the Balance Board. A wispy cloud blocked the sun, and Frankie's mood darkened even more.

Cleo's little prank still stung. "Why would Cleo stuff that ballot box with my name? I thought we were friends. I saw her standing by the table, but I never thought she'd…" *Never thought she'd what? Doom a friend to sitting in a stuffy room, making posters and organizing bake sales? Cleo is capable of anything, especially when someone outfriends her by nine whole people.*

Brett reached into the pocket of his ink-stained jeans. He gave the peasant-skirted hippie chick behind the cart some bills and handed Frankie the button she'd been eyeing. Frankie smiled her thanks and pinned the button to the strap of her sandal.

Brett twirled his skull ring. "You'll be great with all that board stuff. You love getting involved."

"That was before."

"Before what?" Brett asked, serious. "This?" He gestured to a group of girls sifting through their shopping bags, gushing over one another's purchases. "There's more to life than clothes. You made a difference."

Suddenly irritated, Frankie pulled her hand away. "I *tried* to make a difference. Been there, botched that. I freaked everyone out and made all the RADs go into hiding. Clawdeen's the one who changed everyone's mind. I thought it would be me, but it wasn't. Maybe I was built for other things. Like just being a normal teenager and having fun."

"You opened everyone's mind way before Clawdeen's party.

They wouldn't have taken off their disguises if you hadn't been there, reminding them that they could." Brett paused to control his rising voice. "I dunno, I think the Balance Board might be fun...maybe. You could raise money for those portable amp stations you're always talking about. We can build a monster museum, which I will curate, of course...."

Frankie couldn't help smiling. There was a time when that would have sounded like fun—working with a group to make things better. But times change. And so did she.

She sighed and then walked into H&M. A wave of air-conditioning sent a shiver up her back.

"Hey there! Need help finding anything?" asked a girl with a red mohawk and a unibrow.

"Just brows-ing," Brett joked.

Frankie smacked him for being mean. Then she giggled.

Unibrow began refolding cargo shorts.

"I'll never have time to see you if I'm on that board," Frankie whined.

"What if I do it with you?" Brett offered.

She looked at him. He was still leaning against the mirrored column and still smiling.

"You can't. You weren't picked."

"I'll say I was."

"But you weren't."

Brett put his hands on his hips. "Then I'll lie."

Frankie wasn't sure if she should shock him or kiss him. "But—"

"But what?" he asked, flipping through a rack of polka-dot skirts. "Are you really going to stop me from helping our school?"

"What about all the people who didn't get on the board? It's not fair."

"They don't care," Brett insisted. "They were just looking for one last application booster before the summer break."

"How do you know?" Frankie asked, suddenly offended by his cynicism. Didn't anyone want to do the right thing just to do it? Not that she really cared.

"Because that's the reason I applied," he confessed while folding a crumpled pink sweater.

Frankie giggle-gasped. "You what?"

"Heath and I did it together on a dare. Kind of like a Russian roulette thing, but with boring after-school programs instead of bullets. Turns out we both got picked." He pointed a finger gun at his head and fired. "Pow."

Frankie cracked up right there in the middle of the summer sweater section. "When were you going to tell me?"

"I wasn't." He stuck his hands in his pockets. "I was going to surprise you."

Frankie felt electrified all over again. Maybe Brett was right. Maybe it wouldn't be so bad. At the very least, it would give them more time to hang out.

"It'll be fun," he said, coaxing her toward the exit.

"Really?" Frankie beamed.

Brett shrugged. "Anything's better than tennis."

CHAPTER SIX
ROCK BLOCKED

Melody closed her eyes behind her black drugstore sunglasses. She curled her toes in the grass and reached for Jackson's hand. The sun on her face and the burble of the river lulled her like her mother's white-noise sleep machine. Every muscle in her body felt as if it were made of butter, melting into the turquoise-and-brown-striped blanket. In her half-asleep state, she heard a musical jingle over the tinny tune of the River-front carousel. The tinkling sound grew louder and faster. Her nostrils were filled with...a musty, slightly rank odor? *Jackson! Ew!*

She decided to go with it. If love was blind, it should be oblivious to bad smells, too, right?

Oof! A weight like an anvil crash-landed on her relaxed abs. A hot tongue swiped drool across her cheek. Blind and oblivious, maybe, but impervious to pain?

"Jackson!"

"What?" he asked lazily.

"Ahhhhh!" she yelled, bolting up. A damp yellow Lab stole another lick.

"No, Sadie!" called a plump blond woman in a white track-suit. She held a frayed leash as she panted across the grass.

"You thought that was me?" asked Jackson, shielding his eyes from the afternoon sun.

"If the breath fits..." Melody joked.

Jackson pulled the dog toward him. "Funny, 'cause if I closed my eyes, I'd swear these hairy legs were yours."

Melody threw back her head and laughed as Sadie sucked up their lunch scraps like a DustBuster.

"I'm so sorry! She gets so excited when she sees picnics." The woman tugged on the leash, and Sadie trotted off.

"No problem!" they called after her.

"Looking good, Carver," Jackson said, pointing to Melody's white V-neck, which was spotted with muddy paw prints. Turkey and brownies were smeared into their Mexican wool blanket.

"Feeling good, Jekyll." She smiled, making fish lips and strik-ing a pose.

They giggled. Jackson pushed his floppy brown bangs off his forehead. He picked a yellow dandelion from the grass and tucked it behind Melody's ear. She smiled her thanks and flopped onto her back. A gold-tipped feather drifted from her hair and landed beside them. It was a perfect day. But most days spent with Jackson were.

"Remember when we met?" she asked, rolling onto her side to face him. "You were sitting on that bench over there."

His hazel eyes searched the sky. "Nope, not really."

She smacked his leg with a half-eaten drumstick.

"Of course I remember." He sat up halfway. Not an inch of belly

57

fat folded over the top of his ink-stained jeans when he pulled her toward him. "Candace was wearing that crazy silver jumpsuit-y thing. She looked like a total alien, and you were so...pretty."

"Your abs are so chimichanga," she said, inches away from his lips.

"Huh?"

"Hot and slightly disturbing," she answered, borrowing one of Candace's pickup lines. It felt like trying on a stranger's wet bathing suit. "Seriously. How do you even get them like that?"

Jackson sat upright. Melody fell on her side.

He blushed. "When did you start noticing abs? You're not turning into one of *those* girls, are you?"

"What girls?" Melody asked, even though she knew. He was talking about the superficial set who skipped school to shop, compared bodies in the three-way mirrors, and then complained about their thighs over latte lunches. Jackson couldn't tolerate them. To him, Melody was more grounded than a busted airplane. Dependable and wise, she was the last person to abandon her morals and beliefs for something fleeting and trendy. He liked it that way. And she liked that he did.

Jackson picked up his blue-and-white portable hand fan and turned it on. His eyes shut behind his black-framed geek-chic glasses. Melody pushed the fan closer to his slightly sweaty face. When he started to perspire, his corrupt DNA triggered the emergence of D.J., his super-fun but highly irresponsible alter ego. And she didn't want anyone or anything to ruin their day.

"Do you love me because I'm...normal?" she asked, not quite sure how she wanted him to answer.

He opened his eyes and smiled. "Um, I would hardly call you

normal." He plucked a feather from her hair and blew it into the breeze.

"Siren thing aside, I'm boringly predictable. And you're...not. It's like, the minute you sweat, you change into D.J. So maybe you like me because I'm the opposite of that. I never change."

"Wait. You're the one who got up onstage the other night and sang to a bunch of strangers, and I'm the unpredictable one?" Jackson pulled her back down. His short-sleeved plaid button-down smelled like pine-scented deodorant. "You're not dating D.J., are you?"

She giggled, but in a way he was right. Melody was used to thinking she was predictable because, compared to her sister, she always had been. But her performance the other night was just the opposite of predictable. In fact, it was the most spontaneous thing she'd done in years.

"There are a million reasons why we work." He reached for her Tupperware and popped open the lid. "One of them is your brownies." A chocolate crumb landed on the pearly top button of his shirt. She wiped it away. Whatever the reason, he was right—they were a great team.

Melody rolled onto her back and grabbed his hand. As her mind drifted back to Corrigan's, the earthy scent of the sunny afternoon was replaced by sour bar smell...the heat of the spot-light...the rush of energy she got from standing on the stage, her voice soaring, the crowd cheering....Melody sat up and took a sip from her bottle of water. "What are we going to do this sum-mer? That's the real question."

Jackson pushed his bangs off his face. "Actually..." He searched inside his backpack while Melody watched a family in a yellow

59

kayak float past. They seemed so peaceful and satisfied—emotions she had yet to feel in her own life. Not that she wasn't happy with Jackson; she was. But there was a vibration just below the surface of her skin. A restless hum. A tune that moved her, but never to that place that brought her peace. Until the night before. Until she sang.

A glossy brochure appeared in front of her face. The cover featured kids on a wooden stage surrounded by lush forest. "Camp Crescendo!"

"Huh?"

Jackson grinned. "The camp needs counselors."

"But it's, like, the best performing-arts camp in the country. I'm sure there's a waiting list a mile long for jobs."

Jackson leaned back on his elbows. "There is. But my mom knows the staff director. You and I have interviews next Thursday after school—you for musical theater, me for art. Imagine, two months at a sleepaway camp. No school, no parents, no tragic Applebee's uniform."

And so she did….Dawn hikes to mist-covered peaks. Midnight swims. Holding hands under a blanket during campfire sing-alongs. Crickets, stars, musical theater. If she had to get a summer job—which she did—this was a more-than-decent option. "It's great!" She leaned toward him for a thank-you kiss when—*ping!*

Melody pulled back to check her phone.

To: **Melody**
June 4, 2:57 PM
CANDACE: @ SHANE'S DORM. GRUNGE GODDESS AUDITIONING LEAD SINGER. SIGNED U UP. NEXT THURS. 3:30 @ SHERWOOD SUITE #503. BEST SISTER EVER OUT!

Melody shaded the screen and read it again. And again. And again... She jumped to her feet and hopped barefoot in the grass. "Yessssss!"

"What?" Jackson asked, standing up and hopping too.

"GrungeGoddessisauditioningnewsingersandCandacegotme onthelist! I have an audition next week!"

He high-fived her. "Maybe you can you do something about that name."

Melody froze. *Did he really just say that?*

"Sorry...it's great news. It really is," he said, snickering.

Icicles formed inside Melody where warm syrupy love had flowed only moments earlier. She dumped the brownies into the trash. "Way to rock block."

"Not the brownies!" Jackson screeched.

"You're next if you don't watch it," she said, only half-joking.

"I just can't get over the name. It's so...dorky."

"You would know," she said, pointing at his misbuttoned shirt.

"I'm just kidding," he said with a chuckle. "I'm really happy for you. Maybe now I'll get to see you perform." Jackson cranked his fan up to high. He held it in front of his face with one hand and squeezed her bare calf with the other.

Melody lowered the fan so she could see his eyes. "Does this mean you'll come to the audition?"

"Depends."

Melody waited.

"I want a new batch of brownies by sundown."

"Deal," she said, holding out her hand.

"Deal," he said, shaking it. "When is the audition?"

She reread the text. "Thursday at three thirty."

"Uh-oh."

Another rock block.

"Our camp interviews are at five."

Melody tucked a dandelion behind Jackson's ear. "That gives us an hour and a half. We'll be fine."

He looked down at the grass. Melody squeezed his hand, using all of her willpower not to use her voice on him. Because how easy would that be? *Jackson, listen up. You're going to support me on all things music-related. And you're gonna love it.*

To which he would reply, *Yes, Melly. Whatever you say, Melly. Can I carry you onstage, Melly?*

To which she would reply, *Blech!*

Because honestly, if she wanted a robo-boyfriend, Mr. Stein could probably stitch one up for her by Monday. She needed to know that Jackson's support came of his own free will. Without that, she'd never know if—

"I'm in!"

"Perfect!" Melody jammed her phone into the back pocket of her cutoff jean shorts and grabbed her canvas purse. "Come on. I have to start practicing!"

Jackson tossed the remaining plastic containers into the basket and hooked his backpack over his shoulder.

"I guess the picnic's over."

CHAPTER SEVEN
T'EAU-DALLY DISSED

Clawd speared a piece of teriyaki tofurkey, reached across the teak table, and fed a bite to Lala.

"Mmmmm..." She licked her lips, savoring the flavor of salty meat substitute. "Now you," she said, feeding a bite to Clawd.

He chewed. "Rabid good! So much better than the real thing."

The undulating sea rocked their yacht like a newborn's cradle. Mr. D popped the cork on a bottle of Martinelli's as Lala leaned back in her deck chair, offering herself to the sun. Her black-and-silver bikini was still damp from their swim with the dolphins. Clawd knelt before her, holding a robin's-egg blue box and wearing a loving grin. Her father stood above them with a camera. Mr. D took off his Carrera sunglasses, allowing a tear of joy to roll freely down his cheek. It was the first time Lala had ever seen him hold a camera, let alone cry with joy. Just as Lala was about to open the blue box, the wind picked up. Clouds rolled in and covered the sun. The sails creaked in protest as the gentle rocking became more of an impatient shake....

"…I *said*, time for uppies. You're late." Uncle Vlad's blue-and-white-checked shirt was covered by a navy apron.

Lala sat up and pulled off her black satin sleep mask. "Huh?" The menagerie of stray animals jumped down to the rug.

Vlad was hunched over her coffin-canopy bed, shaking the frame.

She rubbed her eyes and glanced at the clock by her bed. It was blinking 12:00. "What happened?" she groaned as her balding mouse, Smoked Buddha, darted under the bed before she let the bat in. "What time is it? Why didn't my alarm go off?"

"Your father's tanning bed blew a fuse. Again. All the power went out. Again."

It was hard to believe he would greet her at the breakfast table like a normal father. Hard to believe he had slept in his coffin last night. Hard to believe they would be looking at each other in the flesh and not in high-def. Unless… *What if I dreamed him too?*

"Vite, vite!" Vlad opened the heart-shaped windows and let Count Fabulous in. The bat, dressed in miniature flight goggles and pink glitter-specked faux-fur wing covers, flapped to his perch and assumed his upside-down position. Lala removed his night gear, slipped a tiny satin sleep mask over his eyes, kissed him good day, and then flopped back down. "Ugh! I was having the best dream."

"Well, now you can have the best time getting dressed. Make like *DWTS* and get a move on," he said on his way out the door.

Lala kicked off her pink-and-black satin duvet. Her father had been home for four days, and her pets were still acting as if he were going to eat them for lunch. The day before, she had to carry Teeny Turner down the stairs and force her outside. Apparently the pooch preferred to wee on the carpet rather than risk running into Mr. D . . . as if he'd actually suck the blood of a *stray*. If only they knew who they were dealing with. "Your father feeds on only the finest breeds," he loved to say.

He also loved to pressure her about the future, but so far he hadn't said a word. What if the strays were right? Maybe he had finally lowered his standards. Maybe he was ready to act like a bat and just hang.

Lala wiggled into a red cashmere pullover, black leggings, and knee-high boots. All the other girls were wearing tank tops and summer dresses, but when she'd tried a plum cotton cardigan, she'd spent the entire day shivering. She brushed her fangs and applied a quick spray of lily-of-the-valley perfume. A swipe of clear lip gloss and a coat of mascara, and this vamp was ready for an old-fashioned family breakfast.

Pungent beef smells filled the lower level of the house and were now making their way upstairs. Still, nose to perfumed wrist, Lala managed to push through. Probably some weird blood sausage or kidney pie thing her dad had imported from Europe. The thought made her empty stomach churn. Still, dry heaves were a small price to pay for having him back in her life.

"Morning, Daddy!" Lala called, entering the black-and-white kitchen. Uncle Vlad insisted on a checkerboard floor and bright marble countertops to avoid chopping his fingers off — an inevitability if he were forced to slice and dice in the dark. Mr. D eventually gave in. When it came to cuisine, Vlad called the shots. A reasonable compromise for gourmet, her father said. Lala plugged her nose. How much for a giant fan to suck out the meat smell?

"I don't want excuses; I want results," her father said, rising from the leather office chair he had obviously relocated to the breakfast table. He always looked like a Hugo Boss model: dark, gelled, and dressed in a fitted suit at places to which others wore sweats. "If he can't raise the funds by Monday, I'm going to—" He glanced at Lala and then switched to Romanian.

"Hi, Daddy," Lala tried again. As she reached for his cold hand, he held up a finger and continued his high-decibel conversation while beating the keys of his laptop. Embarrassed, she grinned at Musclavada, the dark-suited bodyguard standing nearby. Muscles (as Lala and Vlad secretly called him) nodded in reply.

"What's going on?" she asked Vlad, who was seated at the table. The Belgian waffles were covered with documents. The muffin basket had been shoved aside to make room for a portable fax machine. And three international cell phones rested on Lala's empty plate.

"Whatever could you mean?" asked her uncle in mock shock, obviously annoyed. "We always toss office equipment onto our breakfast." He scraped almond butter onto Lala's cinnamon raisin bagel as if trying to spark a flame.

"Not so hard, it's gonna—" Just then the bagel slipped from his angry grip and landed facedown on a black marble square.

"Looks like you're Os," Lala joked, trying to lighten the mood. "My turn." She made an X out of two tofu sausages and placed them on a white floor tile.

Vlad threw his hands in the air. "Fabulous! Just fabulous!"

The Count, thinking he had been summoned for a meal, swooped in, scooped up the bagel, and flew back upstairs. Vlad knocked his head against the juicer while Lala tried her hardest not to laugh.

66

"It's okay," she said, reaching past her uncle for her white mug. "A soy latte is all I wanted, anyway."

"I hope you like it cold," Vlad mumbled from the side of his mouth. "Thanks to my brother—the tan-pire—there is a state-of-the-art tanning bed in my meditation room, and it blew half the fuses in this house." He handed Lala a twenty-dollar bill. "Hit the drive-through Starbucks."

Lala tucked the money in the side of her boot as her father paced the kitchen, his guttural Romanian becoming louder and angrier. "Isn't this great?"

Vlad pressed a finger on his twitching eyelid. "What?"

"We're like a real family."

"Gresit!" Mr. D charged out of the kitchen. His voice boomed down the hallway toward the foyer. Muscles slipped out behind him.

Vlad rolled his eyes. "Would it kill them to clear their plates?" Pushing the laptop to the far end of the table, he jabbed at the power button on the remote, muted the flat screen, and then pulled the plastic off a brand-new issue of *Architectural Digest*. He flipped through the first few pages of furniture ads and then looked up. "The tanning bed. The moisturizers. The staff. The luggage. The heat lamps...He hung a satin robe over the Whitmore!"

Lala gasped. She knew what that mirror meant to him. According to the book he'd written—*Fang Shui: Decorating Tips for Vampires in Need of Positive Qi*—the mirror was located where the heart corner and the wealth corner merged. Meaning it was supposed to help Uncle Vlad attract a wealthy lover. Unless it was covered. Which meant he would die poor and alone.

67

"He's probably not going to stay very long, anyway. He never does," Lala offered. The realization brought a hopeful grin to Vlad's face. And turned Lala's blood to stone. Would she ever be good enough to stay put for?

"I'd better go," she said, desperate to hit Starbucks before first period.

A chirping sound came from her microfiber bag. Lala and Vlad exchanged a glance. "Probably someone needing a ride." She shrugged.

Blocked.

Vlad sighed and then returned to his magazine.

She blew a good-bye kiss to Vlad and answered her phone. "Hullo?"

"Ahhhh. *Oui*. Ehhh, Lala?" It was a heavily accented female voice. Probably another one of her father's foreign girlfriends trying to get in good with the daughter, a story older than she was.

Lala pushed through the saloon doors. "Um-hmm?" Whoever it was would have to talk to her on her way to school.

"*Je m'appelle* Brigitte T'eau from—"

"And Dickie Dally here. Dally Sports Apparel."

Clawd? Lala stopped, wondering who could be punking her. *He doesn't even know about the T'eau Dally—*

The woman with the accent cut back in.

"*Votre* e-mail *était rempli de passion et*—"

"A real home run, Slugger. You're one of our three T'eau Dally finalists. Well, really, you're our favorite, but we're not allowed to say that or the suits will get pissed. Ha!" he boomed, and then cough-cleared his throat. "I'm thinkin' Frenchie and I will swing

68

by and see you first....Let's see...maybe...Thursday the twenty-third? Hey, B, is Thursday *bueno* for *vous*?"

"*Mais oui*," answered the woman, her silken cashmere voice a welcome change from his rough poly blend. "Please, uh, Dickie, call me Brigitte."

"Super! Okay, huddle up. Here's the game plan: We'll scope out the school, make sure it's not haunted—ha!—and acquaint ourselves with the freaks that are gonna rep our new shoe. The sicker the better. Ugly'll work too. Ha! Blame that *Jersey Shore* show—gritty's the new glossy." He coughed and then spit. "I mean, who ever would have thought that Dickie Dally would merge with some uptight European broad? Ha!"

Okay, Clawd would never say "broad." One time he called her "babe" in front of his football buddies, and she popped his pigskin with her fangs. This was dead real! Lala felt floaty and heavy at the same time, like an anchor being pulled through choppy waters. She waved frantically, trying to get Uncle Vlad's attention.

He tossed his magazine. *What?* he mouthed. "Tell me! Who is it?"

Lala waved again, this time urging him to be quiet. But that only made him mouth *what?* even more.

"Lala?" She heard a different male voice on the line.

"Uh, yes?"

"I'm Red, Mr. Dally's assistant. He had to jump onto another call. And it seems as though we've lost Ms. T'eau to a bad connection. Anyhoo, congratulations on being a finalist!" He sounded Midwestern, like Dickie, but in a less coarse, more cottony way.

A giant smile spread across Lala's face. "Thanks." She giggled shyly. And then to Vlad she mouthed, *T'eau Dally!*

He began jumping up and down, his hands clasped together in thanksgiving. "My fang shui worked! It worked! I moved the laptop into your success corner, and it worked."

"Shhhhhhh," Lala hissed, still smiling.

"Okay, now jot this down," said Red.

Lala grabbed her deep purple lip liner and rolled up her sleeve. "Ready…"

1 of 3 finalists…Thurs @ 12ish…I must pik couple 2 present to DD and BT…if win will get national ad camp… If we win, renamed toe-dally high…1 mill bucks ☺ ♥ ☺ ♥ ☺ ♥

"Got it. Okay. Thanks. See you Thursday." Lala disconnected the call and tossed her phone onto the cracked-leather ottoman. "I'm a finalist! They like me the best! I did it!"

She shouted loud enough for her father to hear. But the only one who rushed to her side was Uncle Vlad. He pulled her into a sandalwood-scented hug and took her with him on his invisible trampoline. She couldn't wait to tell her father. If winning a contest and getting a million-dollar donation for her school didn't prove her worthy of a future, nothing would.

"Me and Clawd are going to represent the T'eau Dally merger in a national ad campaign!" she announced while jumping.

"Eeeeeee!" squealed Uncle Vlad.

"I know!" she squealed back, delighting in the perfection of it all.

A werewolf and a vampire. Did it get more merge-y than that? They were T'eau-Dal opposites. Furry and freezing. Meaty and lean. Pack man and lone girl. She imagined the shoot....*A limousine pulls up to a studio in midtown Manhattan. The driver jumps out to open the door. Her pale, stockinged leg emerges. Lala steps out wearing a violet wrap and Harry Winston diamonds. Mr. D is waiting on the sidewalk as a sunglassed and mohawked Clawd emerges. In the studio, makeup artists decide their job is pointless—Lala's so beautiful already. Stylists agree that her own clothes are better than anything they could have pulled. Mr. D turns off his phone and unclips his earpiece, not wanting to miss a second of this experience. He sips Perrier as he watches his daughter, in awe of her fabulousness. Lala and Clawd pose against a soft gray backdrop. The camera clicks. They're naturals. They take five to look at the proofs... but only Clawd is there....*

Lala stopped jumping. Vampires don't show up in photographs—hence the blank box above Lala's name every year in the Merston High yearbook and the *Where were you on photo day?* caption below it. Oh, well. Her father wouldn't let a simple thing like that get in the way, and so neither would she. She'd just have to find someone else.

Muscles entered the drawing room, followed by Mr. D, who shouted a final few Romanian words into the cell phone before jabbing his finger at it to end the call.

"Dad! You're never going to believe who just called!" she chirped the instant he hung up.

He began texting. "Hmmm?"

She blocked his path. "Guess!"

71

He stopped just before crashing into her and finally met her dark eyes. Lala raised her eyebrows and flashed him a full-fanged smile.

"Draculaura, I don't have time for games. What is it?"

Lala's smile faded. But only for a second. He was going to be so proud.... "I won this contest, for Merston, and—"

His BlackBerry beeped. "I have a call. Later, okay?"

Uncle Vlad gasped.

"But—"

Mr. D glared at Muscles, who stepped forward and lifted Lala out of the way. The duo then hurried by and entered the kitchen.

Lala rolled down her sleeve and slid on her sunglasses. There was no fanging way she'd let her dad see her cry.

Ping.

TO: Lala
June 8, 8:11 AM
FRANKIE: WHERE R U? WE R LATE!

Lala kissed Uncle Vlad on the cheek, grabbed her car keys, and let the door slam shut behind her. She'd rather tell Frankie the good news, anyway. She might spark. But she'd never bite.

CHAPTER EIGHT

ON YOUR MARKS…
GET SET…T'EAU!

Frankie's outfit was no accident. One look at her yellow
tennis skirt and white warm-up jacket, and the Balance Board
members would assume she had a match after school. And, in
the name of consideration, might hurry things along (unlike the
board's first meeting, which had lasted two hours and nine minutes). But so far, not so good. Frankie had been in the school's
chemical-scented bio lab—*like I don't smell that enough at
home!*—for fifteen minutes, and the meeting hadn't even started.
So much for subliminal dressing. The only one who noticed her
outfit was Ghoulia, and that's because Frankie had left the price
tags on.

"Order! I bring this meeting to order!" called Haylee Barron-
Mendelwitz, slamming a gold-plated gavel (a gift to her father
from his law firm).

Frankie was one minute closer to freedom. All she had to do
was announce Lala's great news and then—

"Before we get down to business," said Haylee, reaching

behind her floral jumper and pulling out a plastic container, "let's make sure our blood sugar is up. Some homemade flaxseed-and-cranberry-oat bars?" Haylee began handing out the brown blocky things with the urgency of a Red Cross volunteer.

Ever since Bekka (Haylee's former social overlord/Brett's vengeful ex-girlfriend) transferred to Whitmore High, Haylee had come out of her shell like a molting crab. No longer forced to live in the shadows, she sought the spotlight. But not the fun kind that comes with wardrobe stylists and hair and makeup teams. More like the bossy spotlight, which tended to be fluorescent and not very flattering.

Heath Burns, her fire-burping boyfriend, took two bars and then passed the plate to Jackson, who passed it to Brett, who passed it to Frankie. Frankie took the smallest bar, just to be polite, and handed it to Ghoulia. The zombie eyed the selection. "Mmmmmmm..." she moaned, but didn't take one. She was clearly too smart to bite.

"I'd like to make an announcement," Frankie said.

"Not before we recap." Haylee popped open her green faux-crocodile case and pulled out a legal pad. "First item on the agenda..." She glanced at Heath over her beige glasses. He stood and faced the room. The sleeves on his blue-and-white plaid button-down were too short. His pale wrist bones stuck out like bolts.

"Uh...number one: We agreed that Haylee is chair—"

Frankie giggled. *How can she be a chair?*

Heath continued. "I'm the reporter—"

"It's called a secretary," Haylee corrected.

"That's a girlie title," he insisted. "I like reporter."

Brett snickered. He made a finger gun and pointed it at Heath. *Pow*, he mouthed.

Heath whipped his napkin at Brett. It landed on Brett's desk with a curious thud. He peeled it open to find a half-chewed oat bar. Brett whipped it back, and the two broke into hysterics.

"Order!" Haylee called, slamming her gavel. "Proceed."

It took Heath a few seconds to stop laughing before he could continue. "Frankie is social coordinator, Jackson is creative coordinator, and Brett is the liaison of cool." The guys high-fived in honor of Brett's hard-won title. Frankie beamed. She and her guy had the coolest jobs.

"Ceeee…eeeee…ohhh," moaned Ghoulia.

"Oh, sorry, Ghouls," Heath said, flipping a page in his Megan Fox notebook. "You're CEO—chief executive observer."

"Mmmmmm," she smile-moaned.

Heath continued. "Number two: Haylee moved that we create a peer-counseling corner in the library, where students can talk about assimilation problems. Frankie moved we transition to half-days in June in honor of the summer solstice. Jackson wants to turn the cafeteria walls into giant murals, bump up the air-conditioning, and build a recording studio. And then Frankie said she needed a charge, so we adjourned—" Heath gripped his belly. "Ouch," he moaned.

"What is it?" Haylee asked, racing to his side.

Heath doubled over. "I think I ate too many nut bars."

Uh-oh!

"Take cover!" Brett shouted. "Fire in the hole!"

Haylee reached for her gear—a fire-retardant backpack filled with an extinguisher, sand, and aloe.

Jackson ran toward the hall. Ghoulia yawned. Frankie shot under her desk. The last thing she needed was for Heath to blow booty and ignite her new tennis outfit. Brett crouched next to her and winked. She blew him a kiss and crossed her fingers.

A blast of heat blew through the room, followed by a blast of foam. The ends of Frankie's hair sizzled, but her skirt stayed intact. *Mint!*

"Sorry, guys. You can come out now."

Brett and Frankie wiggled out from under their desks and into what had become a winter wonderland. Brett's spiky hair was smoking. Jackson reentered slowly, hand fan cranking. Ghoulia had remained seated the whole time, reading her *Dead Fast* graphic novel.

"Nice going," Heath said, high-fiving Haylee. "You got it out before the alarm this time."

Like an outlaw, Haylee blew the remaining foam bits off the hose and stuffed the extinguisher back into the bag. "Beat my best time by nine seconds."

A black crater had melted in the chalkboard behind Haylee's head. She removed her melted orange headband and smoothed her mousy brown bangs. "And now for some exciting news…" she began.

Frankie stood and smiled. "It's more like voltage news."

"Not yet," Haylee hissed, motioning for Frankie to take her seat.

Ghoulia made a noise. It sounded like a laugh being stretched.

"We have been asked by Principal Weeks to host the Senior Luncheon on graduation day," Haylee said. "Quite an honor."

Outside the window, three freshman girls were playing Hacky

Sack on the grass. They were sharing a carton of orange juice and giggling every time one of them missed a shot. What Frankie wouldn't have done to be there with—

"Frankie! Are you even listening?" Haylee snapped.

"Huh?"

"Since you're social coordinator, you'll run lead on the luncheon."

Frankie sparked. Throwing parties was not on the to-do-or die list. Attending them was. "I, um—"

"All right, all right," Haylee said. "I'll do it."

"Really?" Frankie asked, unable to hide her relief.

"If it would make you more comfortable," Haylee said, chewing her bottom lip. If it were a bit, she would have been chomping.

"It would," Frankie said.

Haylee hammered her gavel. "Done. I'll run first position." She crossed one orange Croc over her knee and opened her binder to the section marked SENŠR LUNCHEON. "I was thinking we should do a 'We Are the World' theme. We can have steel drummers playing alongside bagpipers, and we can all be in costumes from different parts of the globe. I have a dirndl, and we can rent—"

Frankie cut her off. "I'm so sorry for interrupting, Haylee, but I move that you all listen to this totally mint piece of news."

Haylee sighed. "Go ahead."

Frankie smoothed out her skirt and stood at a slight angle so Brett got the best glimpse of her calf muscles. "Lala entered Merston in this contest run by T'eau Shoes and Dally Sports—"

Heath held up one of his enormous white basketball sneakers. "I wear Dallys all the time."

"And who doesn't love T'eaus?" Frankie added.

Ghoulia glanced down at her flip-flops. "Oooooooooohs."

Frankie responded with a polite smile and then explained the contest in detail, right down to the "gritty is the new glossy" part. "…and one last thing: If we win, next year Merston will be renamed T'eau Dally High."

Ghoulia busted out laughing and then sent Frankie a text:

TO: Frankie
June 8, 3:07 PM
GHOULIA: TODALLY HIGH! THAT'S TOTALLY FUNNY!

Frankie smiled politely at Ghoulia again.

Jackson shook his head and pushed his floppy bangs out of his eyes. "I don't get it. 'Gritty is the new glossy'? What does that even mean? How is gritty glossy?"

"It's like buying jeans with holes in them," Frankie explained.

"Who does that?" Jackson asked.

Ghoulia sent another text.

TO: Balance Board
June 8, 3:09 PM
GHOULIA: CLEO, CLAWDEEN, BLUE…

"Okay, we get it," Haylee snapped.

Heath chewed on his pencil. "So who's gonna be the couple, since Lala doesn't show up in pictures?"

Frankie grabbed Brett's hand. "La said we'd be perfect."

Haylee's hand shot up with such gusto she knocked the glasses right off her face. Lopsided, they swung from their chain like a broken porch swing. "Heath and I are gritty too."

"Don't you mean glossy?" Jackson asked.

Heath and Brett cracked up.

Haylee ignored them. "A normie girl dating a fire-breathing RAD screams merger. The *Statesman Journal* even has a name for RAD-normie romances. They call it the Double RAmie."

"Brett and I are Double RAmies too," Frankie countered.

Haylee stomped her Croc. "Why should it be you and Brett? What about me and Heath?"

Heath sighed. Brett slumped back in his chair. They finger-gunned themselves in the temple. Ghoulia pulled out her iPhone and started playing Angry Birds.

"Come on, Haylee. We're cute and energetic. Uh, not that you're not, but..." Frankie sparked. "It's just that...we just went shopping, and we have some great new clothes, and...we could win this for the whole school!"

Haylee shook her head emphatically. "There's more to life than being cute and fashionable."

"In modeling?" Brett pressed. Heath, his best friend, couldn't help laughing.

Frankie winked. *Thank you.*

He winked back. *No problemo.*

"Vvvovvv," Ghoulia managed to rev while still playing.

"Good idea," Jackson said. "Let's vote."

"Agreed." Haylee slammed her gavel. "All in favor of me and—"

Slowly Ghoulia lifted her head and met Jackson's eyes. Her

blank stare was illuminated, a candle flickering deep in a cave. She sent another text:

TO: Balance Board
June 8, 3:12 PM
GHOULIA: CLEO AND DEUCE

"What?" Frankie and Haylee burst out in unison.

"They're not even Double RAmies!" Haylee said indignantly.

Jackson stood up and grabbed his blue backpack. "I move that we open this up to everyone. Anyone can run, and next week the whole school can vote."

Frankie clapped her hands. "Fun!"

The board members agreed.

Except Haylee, who stormed out. Heath stormed after her.

Frankie grabbed her racket and smiled. "Tennis, anyone?"

CHAPTER NINE
FROM CAMPUS TO CAMP

Melody poked the elevator button for the fifth floor.

Nothing.

She hit it again. And again and again and again. *Why does everything move so slowly when you're in a hurry?!* She yanked Jackson's wrist up and checked his vintage Rolex—3:34 PM. Four minutes late.

"Is this thing right?"

Jackson reclaimed his wrist. "This *thing* belonged to my father."

"Right, sorry." After another finger-bending press of the button, the number five lit up and the doors wobbled shut.

The previous hour had played out like a straight-to-DVD comedy. She'd blown out of school in plenty of time to run home, change clothes, and make her three thirty audition, though it meant going to the "bathroom" during last period and not going back to class.

As Melody bounded down the stairs from her bedroom at

3:01 PM, her mother stepped out of the kitchen, arms folded across her SOME MAKE DINNER, OTHERS MAKE RESERVATŠNS apron. Her expression was Botox-smooth, but her squint indicated scowling.

Glory launched into a *Shouldn't you be studying instead of running off?* lecture (3:07 PM) just as Candace burst through the door with a purple tube dress she'd just picked up from the dry cleaner's. "Wear this!" Then out came the hairbrush. "And try this."

Melody pushed her way out the front door while explaining that her messy ponytail, Mudhoney tee, and light-wash skinny jeans were fine and that the Grunge Goddesses didn't care what she wore. But Candace, as usual, wouldn't take "fine" for an answer and tackled her sister. Candace was trying to pull off the Converse (3:11 PM) when Melody screamed that she'd take the dress (even though it looked like a sausage casing) and the useless hairbrush and change in the car. But not before she thanked Candace for the newly minted fingernail scratch on her left cheek and her now-trembling vocal cords.

The elevator jerked to a stop on the third floor (3:35 PM).

Seriously?

The doors opened to reveal a dimly lit hallway that smelled like vanilla-scented smoke and skunk. Through the haze, a couple—she in overalls and he in a tie-dyed tee—stepped in, giggling.

Overalls poked the button for the first floor repeatedly. "This thing is Smuckers, man."

"Smuckers?" asked her guy.

"Jammed."

82

He snickered while she poked harder.

"We're going up," Melody grumbled.

"Oops. Bad, bad, bad," she told her index finger. She and her heavy-lidded mate burst into hysterics.

Melody rolled her eyes, but Jackson was too intrigued by the flyer-covered walls to feel her frustration.

The elevator came to another abrupt halt, shook, and then settled. Melody yanked Jackson past the cackling couple and crashed into a skinny boy in tight black jeans and a leather vest.

"Sorry."

"Not as sorry as my pathetic audition," he huffed, stomping into the elevator.

Are all college kids this odd?

Melody had always imagined college dorms to be bustling with Top Ramen–eating coeds dressed in study sweats and stressing about some paper that was due in an unreasonable amount of time, their pallid skin proof of the nutrient-sucking rays emanating from their computer screens. She envisioned the cheery decor as a space-saving tribute to the latest IKEA catalog.

Instead, the congested hallway looked more like the hate child of a Paramore concert and an *American Idol* audition. Jittery wannabes—some pacing, most slumped against the cinder-block walls—were either biting their already-bitten nails, side-eyeing the competition, or getting in the zone by humming their audition songs.

Melody took her place at the end of the line, behind a man in a fedora playing a clarinet. "Don't *chick*, *grunge*, and *singer* mean anything to these people?" asked Jackson.

Melody managed to smile in spite of the time (3:38 PM).

Jackson powered up his hand fan. "Man, this place is packed."

He was obviously worried about making it to their camp interview but was too sweet to say it. If he was late because of her, she'd never forgive—*omigod, duh!* "Be right back."

The door to suite 503 was blocked by a redhead seated on a stack of milk crates. Dressed in a preppy white button-down, lime-green capris, and pristine sandals, she was clearly a roommate the rockers were forced to tolerate.

"Um, excuse me," Melody tried in her sweetest voice. Maybe that would be enough.

"No cutting, no matter what," the redhead said, pointing to the black-lipstick lettering on the door that conveyed the same message. Her New York accent was deep-dish thick and probably inherited from a Brooklyn cop.

Melody leaned close to the gatekeeper. Her hair smelled like fruit salad. "You will let me and my boyfriend in next," Melody said softly.

As Melody expected, the redhead's eyelids fluttered. "Just fill out your contact information, and we'll be all set."

From the line, a girl with a purple mohawk asked, "Hey, what was that all about?"

Melody turned to face her. "I'm going in next, and you're so happy for me."

"Cool," said Mohawk, with a generous smile. "Good luck in there."

Melody waved Jackson forward and burst inside the suite before anyone began to riot. It was hardly a graceful entrance, but desperate times…

"Cinderella!" bellowed the girl who had pulled her up onstage at Corrigan's.

Cinderella?

Sage was sitting on the stained gray carpet leaning against a stained mustard-yellow futon, strumming her guitar. Her blue-black hair was stuffed into a floppy green beanie, and her gray mesh shirt hung off one shoulder, revealing the strap of her hot-pink bra. She reached into the mini fridge next to the sofa on which the other two girls were perched. "We would have called you to audition, but you left so fast after the gig at Corrigan's that we didn't even get your name, and you're not in the college directory."

"Oh, sorry. I'm Melody." She waved stiffly and then instantly regretted her dorky awkwardness.

The boxy room had obviously been cleared of beds and dressers to make room for the drum kit, amp, and mini air-hockey table that was piled high with pizza boxes, vending-machine candy wrappers, and soda cans. The stale air smelled like burned microwave popcorn. Melody's pores opened like a fish mouth. It was a good thing Jackson had chosen to wait in the hall. A wind machine would have been his only hope.

The blond stretched out on the futon was elbow deep in a bag of Doritos. Melody recognized the drummer, and not just from the custom sticks in her back pocket. She had a red hibiscus stuck behind one ear, bright blue eyes, and a half shirt that might have been whole on someone who had more ab than flab.

"I'm Nine-Point-Five," the girl said, lifting her hand out of the bag and wiggling her pinkie. The thimble-sized stub was adorned

85

with a thin stack of silver rings. "I'm missing half a finger," she proudly announced. "That's why I'm not a ten."

Melody giggled.

"I'm Cici," said the bass player, sitting on the arm of the sofa and drinking chocolate milk. She wore a tiara in her bleached blond hair and an ivory silk slip dress. Very Courtney L.

"You're making me nervous. Sit down. Relax. We won't bite," Sage said, and then winked at Cici. "At least, I won't."

Melody laughed a little too hard as she sat in a rust-colored armchair. Beside her, an artificial Christmas tree was hung with pairs of broken sunglasses, frayed shoelaces, and scarves. This was like hanging out with the cool version of the popular girls in school—something Melody had yet to experience. There had always been someone to hang out with, but a group? Like this? Never.

Nine-Point-Five sat up. The unapologetic belly bulge that slumped over her jean shorts looked like it had just as much right to be there as the rest of them. It was the first time Melody had ever seen a girl this comfortable in her own skin.

"Those feathers are awesome," Nine said. "Put one on the tree before you leave, will ya? All our friends leave something."

Friends?

Melody plucked out a couple of strays and rested them on the tree branches. "You can have as many as you want."

Sage cracked open a can of grape soda. "So, Melody, what's your deal? You in school? You work? Play guitar?"

Melody stiffened. The interview had begun. She considered using her powers to land the lead, maybe even bestie status. But cutting a line and crossing a line were two totally different things

when it came to destiny. If she cheated, it wouldn't feel reward-
ing. At least, that's what her mother said about people who chose
liposuction over exercise for weight loss.

Melody chose her next words carefully. "I'm still in school. I go
to…" She hesitated. What if Jackson was right, and they thought
she was too young? Melody swallowed. She had to earn this.
And that meant being honest. "I'm a sophomore at Merston
High. I just turned sixteen." She clenched her abs, preparing for
the punch.

Cici adjusted her banana-yellow bra strap. "That's cool. Nine-
Point-Five just turned seventeen."

"You're in high school too?" Melody asked.

"No, I go here. I'm really smart" — she laughed — "or really
stupid."

They all laughed.

"So you like grunge, right?" asked Sage.

That was it? No "We don't hang with high school girls, so get
out"? Melody replayed the conversation in her mind. *I didn't say
anything Siren-y, did I?*

"I love grunge," she said. "I was listening to Nirvana and Hole
back in middle school. The first CD I bought with my own
money was *Pretty on the Inside*." She paused, allowing the swell
of emotion to wash through her. "I went to Beverly Hills High,
and I didn't really fit in. I ate a lot of lunches with my iPod."

Hand in the air, Nine rushed to Melody's side. "I'll high-four-
point-five to that, sistah!" She smacked Melody's palm.

Sage nodded. "Same story for all of us. But Davina, our last
singer, was a total fit-wit."

Huh?

"Obsessed with fitting in."

"Not with us, though," explained Cici. "With the quote un-quote popular crowd."

Melody could have talked to these girls forever. But Jackson was waiting, and she wanted to be fair. "So, who wants to Smucker?"

The trio exchanged puzzled glances.

OMG, what was I thinking? It wasn't even clever when Overalls said it! Melody wanted to charge for the rectangular window and test out her feathers.

"Wait, do you mean *jam*?" asked Sage.

Mortified, Melody nodded. "It's an old roadie term from the seventies," she lied.

"I love it!" said Cici.

"Me too," said Nine-Point-Five, twirling her sticks. "Let's Smucker. One, two, one two three four!"

Melody recognized the cover instantly. It was a reggae-slash-punk-infused version of "Everlong" by the Foo Fighters.

"Join in whenever," Sage called over the music.

Melody stood and closed her eyes. She tapped her thigh to the offbeat and then began.

"Come down and waste away with me..."

She sang quietly at first, blending, not showcasing. But when the sunny beat cooled, Melody fused with the song. The music rose up through the floor, into her high-tops, up her legs, through her stomach, and out her mouth like a hot spring.

The redhead poked her head in and began swaying. Behind her, wannabes craned for a glimpse inside. Melody saw them as if in a dream. Gauzy and distant. There but indistinguishable.

"If anything could ever feel this real forever, if anything could ever be this good again…"

The final line hung in the air like Candace's Black Orchid perfume. The acoustic bass and guitar chords quieted. Everything went silent. The redhead closed the door with a soft click.

"Woooo-hooooo!" howled Nine-Point-Five, waving her sticks in the air.

Cici tossed up her tiara and shouted, "That rocked!"

Melody burst into laughter.

"So, what are your summer plans?" asked Sage, unplugging.

Melody checked to see that the door was closed all the way. "Um, no plans yet," she muttered. "Why?"

"We're trying to line up gigs so we don't have to get jobs."

Thoughts of warm summer nights and stage-hopping gave Melody roller-coaster stomach. *What could be better?*

An urgent knock interrupted. Jackson entered.

"Who's the accountant?" Nine whisper-asked Cici.

The fuzzy love screen that had covered Melody's eyes whenever she looked at her boyfriend lifted, and she saw Jackson the way the Goddesses must have seen him. His freshly ironed short-sleeved plaid button-down was tucked too neatly into his pleated khakis. His soft brown bangs were gelled and combed across his forehead, and his black glasses were definitely more geek than chic. It was the first time she'd ever looked at him like this.

"Uh, sorry, Carl, the tax club only meets on Saturday," said Sage.

Jackson glared at Melody.

"Um…everyone, this is my, uh, Jackson."

Sage, Cici, and Nine-Point-Five stared at her. Nine-Point-Five glanced at Jackson and then back at Melody as if to say, *For real?*

Jackson looked at Melody. Hurt carved an invisible path between them. Was she that insecure?

"Sorry to interrupt, but it's four fifteen and—"

Melody widened her eyes. *Five more minutes?*

Jackson widened back. *You promised.*

Nine-Point-Five broke the heavy silence. "Hey, I know you! You're that guy from the 'Ghoul' show!" She tapped Sage's shoulder with her sticks. "Remember him?"

Sage nodded, recognition spreading across her face. "Yeah!"

Melody stood reluctantly and joined Jackson at the door.

Nine-Point-Five followed her. "I loved you in that show! Can you actually turn into that fun guy, or was that whole thing faked?"

Melody exhaled.

Jackson smiled gratefully. It wasn't often that his alter ego inspired such admiration. "It's all real," he said, flashing his hand fan.

"That's hot!" Nine-Point-Five said. "We were calling you Brad Pitt-Stain because you were all sweaty."

Jackson managed a smile. Melody blushed on his behalf.

"It was nice meeting you. Your band is really good." Jackson flashed them an earnest thumbs-up. And then to Melody, "Come on, we have to go."

She turned and looked back into the room. Sage smiled a disappointed half smile. "Hey, if you've got somewhere better to go…"

Melody shook her head. "No, it's not that. It's just—"

"Actually, we've got summer job interviews at a performing-arts camp," he explained, the way someone might brag about walking the red carpet.

The room was silent. Cici and Nine burst out laughing.

"So you do have summer plans," Sage noted, confused.

"Not really," Melody said, avoiding Jackson's eyes. "I mean—"

"No problem," Sage said, looking away.

Melody swallowed. "Okay, well thanks so much. That was awesome. Talk to you later, I guess?"

Jackson led her into the elevator like a petulant preschooler.

Maybe not telling them she was a Siren had been a mistake. Maybe it was her destiny to use her voice, not to hide it. Maybe...

Bing.

The door closed behind them.

"Going down?" asked a chipper girl with an eager-to-please smile.

Jackson nodded.

Melody sighed. *Going down, indeed.*

CHAPTER TEN
ACCESS D-NIED

The cafeteria, which smelled like wet wool beanies and tuna casserole, crackled with cutthroat competition. It was the first time Lala had been responsible for anything cutthroat in her entire life, and it felt surprisingly good.

An unfamiliar warm feeling—was it pride?—filled her like soft serve in a cone. It tickled her insides and made her hold her head up high and flash her fangs at everyone who passed. Both RADs and normies were excited about the possibility of being sponsored by two of the biggest footwear brands on the planet. And her dad would be, too, if he ever hung up his headset long enough to hear about the contest.

A red plastic tray of cheeseburgers floated by, followed closely by a lavender raincoat belted with a delicate silver chain.

"Hey, Spectra!"

The ghost obviously hadn't heard her over the lunchtime playlist's latest Jack Johnson selection, because the cheeseburgers kept moving. "Spectra!"

A girl in a denim jacket appeared in Lala's path. "Who are you voting for? Cleo or Frankie? Maybe just give us the first initials or something if you don't want to take sides."

Lala opened her mouth to respond, but a cool lilac breeze blew in her ear. She shivered.

"You called?"

Lala turned toward Spectra's sweet, ethereal voice—and found herself facing a vintage Pac-Man tee and khaki cargo shorts. "Billy? I just saw Spectra. Is she okay?"

"It's me. Spectra."

Lala paused, confused.

"Billy and I decided to switch clothes today. That way I could take his English test, and he could take my bio quiz."

"Must be nice," Lala mumbled.

The girl in the denim jacket had turned back to her friends. "I'm telling you, Cleo might dress the best, but Frankie's so authentic."

Lala said she was undecided and then headed toward her usual table.

Haylee and Heath took up one corner, flipping back and forth between the SENŠR LUNCHEON and T'EAU DALLY sections of her Balance Board binder. Haylee's mousy bangs looked greasy, and she had bags under her eyes. Clearly, campaigning for T'eau Dally while planning the senior graduation luncheon was more than her looks could handle.

Frankie, Blue, and Clawdeen were hovering over a magazine, looking for vote-day outfits. Lala grinned and slid onto the bench next to Clawd, who was too engrossed in Deuce's update on last night's winning basket to notice.

Cleo took advantage of the lull in the sports recap to wave

papyrus samples in front of Deuce's nose. Were they planning a campaign or a wedding? He shrugged and pointed to the middle one, though his mirrored Ray-Bans made it impossible to know if he was even looking. Lala couldn't help wondering how much he needed his glasses versus how much he hid behind them. Yes, without something covering his eyes, everything Deuce looked at would turn to stone. But contact lenses could be coated with the same solution that kept his shades from transforming onlookers. Contacts just wouldn't conceal his intolerance for girlie stuff.

"Howzit with the boomer being back?" Blue stretched out her webbed fingers and pinched a piece of *unagi* with her chopsticks.

Lala grinned, hoping the fake fang flash conveyed more confidence than she actually felt. Leave it to Blue to remember to ask about the "amazing" father-daughter relationship Lala had been blabbing about all week. How they had spent hours bonding by the fire, rising and shining for early-morning hikes, cooking vegan meals together...Because how could she actually admit that her father had been home for two weeks and they'd barely even talked? That her pets were terrified of him? That he had no idea about the T'eau Dally contest?

Thankfully, she never had to. Arcade Fire's "Wake Up" faded just in time for the entire table to hear Jackson whine, "Come on, Melly, you've been on that thing all day!"

"I promised Sage I'd send her the name of a bootleg."

Jackson took a bite of his turkey on rye. Melody sent her text.

"Speaking of bootleg, have you seen the new Mother jeans?" Cleo asked. "They are a perfect mix of flare and skinny. I'm sending Ram out for a pair after school if anyone wants to place an order."

94

Clawdeen raised her hand.

"Speaking of perfect mix," Spectra said, "I think Billy and I should try out for the T'eau Dally thing. We're the perfect combination of beautiful and gorgeous."

Everyone cracked up.

Cleo flicked her on the arm. "Dumb and dumber is more like it."

Billy unscrewed the top on Cleo's chili powder shaker. As usual, she reached for the spice and shook. A hailstorm of red powder coated her tabbouleh.

"*Ka*, Billy!" She pinched the eye of Horus amulet around her neck and waved it in the air. She snapped the lids back onto the glass containers of her Middle Eastern feast and dropped them into her linen tote. "Come on, D."

Deuce shrugged and popped the last bite of his pepperoni pizza into his mouth. He stood, stretched, and grabbed his empty tray, following Cleo as she marched out.

"I'm so over her acting like she's better than the rest of us," Billy said.

"Go easy on her," Frankie said. "She's just upset because her twin sister, Nefra, is leaving Salem for Alexandria."

"Twin?" Lala asked. "They're not twins."

"Yeah, Nefra is older than Cleo," Spectra said. "And where did you hear she was moving? She lives in Cairo."

"You told me that," Frankie said pointedly.

"Me?" Spectra gasped.

Ping.

Ping. Ping. Ping. Ping. Ping.

Ping. Ping.

Like kernels in a microwave, text alerts popped throughout the cafeteria. Clawdeen, Blue, Melody, Jackson, Frankie, Heath, Lala, Clawd, Billy, and Spectra all reached for their phones in unison.

Haylee looked up from her planner.

Brett laughed. "What's that? Like a secret RAD code or something?"

No one responded. The RADs were too busy reading the message that glowed from their screens.

TO: ALL
June 14, 12:34 PM
MR. D: MANDATORY MTG 7 PM FRI AT THE CLEARING. RADS ONLY.

Jackson was the first to ask. "What's going on, Lala?"

"Why so mysterious?" asked Heath.

Billy's phone waved in the air. "What's happening?"

Brett and Haylee glanced at each other in a *no fair!* sort of way.

"Why the clearing?" wondered Clawd.

"Why does it have to be Friday?" complained Melody.

Lala's cheeks burned. She had no idea, but she wasn't about to let on. Not after she'd been bragging all week about how close she and her dad were getting.

She made a zipping motion across her lips in an *of-course-I-know-but-I-can't-tell-you* kind of way.

Clawdeen groaned. "Oh. Come. On! You have to tell us! You can't keep us waiting until Friday."

Lala accidentally locked eyes with Melody. *Great. All I need is for Melody to force me to admit I don't know what's going on.* Lala quickly looked away.

Blue leaned across the table and grabbed an apple slice from Lala's tray. "It's got to be about the T'eau Dally thing. Right, La?"

Lala tried her best to look coy. Not that she really knew what coy looked like.

"I bet the ol' boomer is gonna throw some ace congratulations barbie for Lala," Blue said.

Lala dug her fangs into her bottom lip. The pain distracted her from the torture.

"I know something," Spectra whispered, sending a cool, lilac-scented breeze across the table. Everyone leaned closer to the Pac-Man shirt. "I heard that Mr. D is resigning as our superior. He's holding the meeting to announce the new leader. As soon as he's done, a helicopter will whisk him away to Majorca."

"Who's the new superior?" asked Heath.

"You have a *superior*?" asked Haylee.

Frankie crinkled her brows. "Where's Majorca?"

Lala's legs began to itch. She wanted to race home and beg her father for the truth. What if her dad was going to take her with him, as a surprise? But what if the surprise was that he *wasn't*?

Bwoop. Bwoop. Bwoop.

The bell rang, signaling the end of lunch and the end of Spectra's story.

"Whoops!" She pushed back from the table and got to her feet. Grabbing Billy's old gray messenger bag, she made kissy noises. "Gotta scoot! Don't want to be late for my English test."

Everyone turned to face Lala. She felt the tofu fingers rise up in

her belly and gather in the back of her throat. "I can't say anything," she managed. "He trusted me to keep the secret."

"Come on," they urged.

Lala squirmed uncomfortably.

Clawd elbow-nudged her. His yellow-brown eyes were intense
and focused. "You don't have to tell anyone anything. You're
great at keeping secrets. That's one of the things I…" He stopped
himself in case anyone was listening, but squeezed her hand
under the table.

Clawd was right. She was good at keeping secrets. If only she
had one to keep.

CHAPTER ELEVEN
CAMPAIN IN THE BUTT

TUESDAY, JUNE 14

Bwoop. Bwoop.

School's out. It's T'eau time!

Frankie kissed her flyers for luck and forced an ear-grazing smile. Smiling, she'd read, prompts the secretion of serotonin, nature's happy chemical. And it was crucial she project joy and confidence, especially under such misty skies. She needed to win the heart spaces (and votes!) of her fellow Merstonites. If she didn't, someone else (Cleo! Haylee!) would.

The main doors parted with a slam, and the student tsunami surged. Frankie seratonin-smiled a stitch wider than usual and called, "You won't regret a vote for Frankie and Brett!" She handed her first green flyer to a freshman in glasses. He blushed and then swallowed, his skinny Adam's apple bobbing like a fishing lure. She offered her second flyer to a senior with black clip-on bangs. The girl waved Frankie away like a bad smell. "I'm a de Nile–phile," she announced, flashing the charm on her necklace.

A gift from Cleo, the magic amulet was supposed to bring good fortune to anyone who wore it—if the wearer voted for her and Deuce. Every girl who passed seemed to be wearing one. Stars for fame, coins for wealth, hearts for love…So far, Cleo's charms were doing a great job making Frankie disappear. She hoped Brett was having more luck by the football field.

"STEIN AND REDDING GO TOGETHER LIKE DOGS AND SHEDDING!" she called into the nonresponsive crowd. Classmates hurried by, refusing to make eye contact with her. *Is this how the perfume-sample sprayers at Saks feel? It's only a piece of paper, people!*

Desperate to spread the word, Frankie accidentally passed a flyer to Haylee, who wadded it up and tossed it into the trash.

"Thank you for not littering," Frankie managed in her kindest voice. Because the It Couple weren't just models; they were role models.

"Thank you for killing trees!" Haylee shouted.

Her supporters applauded as if she'd just finished her inaugural address.

Address?

A dress!

That's it!

WEDNESDAY, JUNE 15

If Frankie wanted to look like the ambassador of fusion, she would have to dress like the ambassador of fusion. No more black jeggings and off-the-shoulder shirts. That was expected like the 9:07 AM train to Snoozerville. From now on, she would have Reese's Peanut Butter Cup style: two different tastes blended. Only hers would be sporty and sassy, just like the T'eau Dally brand.

In the first-floor bathroom, Frankie studied her reflection: pink super high-top Chucks, rainbow-striped thigh-high socks, a *Black Swan*–inspired black tutu skirt, a form-flattering Merston football jersey (thanks to Clawdeen's DIY sewing skills and Clawd's generous donation), and a cropped denim blazer. Her hair was tied in dozens of fist-sized knots with colorful shoelaces, and her makeup was runway-ready. *Poor Lala*, she thought. Frankie couldn't imagine a life without mirrors. Color blindness would be bad enough. But couture blindness? It deserved a handicapped parking spot and an annual fund-raiser.

Frankie kissed the mirror, leaving behind a pink pucker, and any last bits of insecurity left over from the day before. She and Brett had a contest to win.

Brett was leaning against a poster-covered wall, waiting for Frankie, when she came out into the hallway. He was wearing the new robin's-egg blue oxford she'd bought for him. It was the last thing anyone would expect to see with his worn black motorcycle jacket and hiking boots. Yes, he too was fusing like a light box, mashing like sweet potatoes, blending like a smoothie.

"There's my peanut butter cup," he joked.

Frankie beamed. Haylee's platform was full of substance, Cleo's full of ancient spells. But Stein and Redding had the image down. This was a print campaign, for bolt's sake. What else was there?

A gaggle of passing girls slowed to check their outfits.

"T'eau-Dally representing Merston's mix!" Frankie told them.

Once the girls were gone, Brett muttered, "You don't think we're going to win this just because we look like Elton John, do you?"

"Brett, image is everything. Look at the Real Housewives of OC, DC, and NYC. They're famous because of their voltage clothes and their fancy houses."

Brett rolled his eyes. "And the fact that they try to claw one another's eyes out."

Frankie groaned in frustration. "All I'm saying is that this is like a game."

"Um, look." Brett pointed to the hand-lettered papyrus banner that stretched from one side of the sophomores' lockers to the other like a beige ecofriendly rainbow.

LEARN FROM THE
MIX-MASTERS

Free Basketball Clinic with Deuce

Nile River Mud Facials with Cleo

Wednesday 3:45 PM

Frankie groaned. "And it looks like the game just changed."

THURSDAY, JUNE 16

Frankie's joints ached. Her fingertips were blistered. Her portable amp purse reeked of flat-ironed Barbie hair. She flopped onto her metal operating table and pulled the fleece-covered electromagnetic blanket over her shoulders. She was beat. Drained. Exhausted. Exhilarated. And finally on her way to the winner's circle.

Rolling onto her side, she looked into the glass aquarium by her bed. "You guys were so right," she told the Glitterati. "It was a megawatt success." Five white rats sprinkled with pink-and-orange glitter stared back, whiskers twitching as if to say, *We told you so*.

"I must have zapped two hundred cell phones today. Those things will hold a charge for weeks. That's got to be good for major votes." She yawned. Ghostface Killah rose to his hind legs and scratched at the glass with pink paws. *I wish I could have helped you*, he tried to convey.

"Len Walsh's car battery died too. So I jump-started it. That alone was probably worth twenty votes."

There was a light rap on the door.

"Come in," Frankie called.

A sliver of light entered the room and then splayed out like a paper fan. "I thought I heard voices. What are you still doing up?" asked her mother. She sat on the edge of the table and stroked her daughter's hair. Frankie inhaled Viveka's rose-scented night cream.

"I was telling the Glitterati about the contest," she said, using the last of her energy to roll onto her back.

"How's it going?"

Frankie yawned. "I'm drained."

"Remind me why it's so important to be this 'It Couple,'" her mother said.

"You get to be in ads and stuff," Frankie answered. "Like real models."

"And . . . ?" asked her mother, as though that wasn't enough.

"And what?"

"And what's so great about that?" Viveka's violet eyes were wide and expectant, ready to take in Frankie's answer without judgment.

"Everyone wants to be a model," Frankie tried. The words came out sounding foreign.

"Why?" asked her mother, wanting to understand.

"Because."

Viveka waited.

"Because being a model means you're pretty and—" She stopped. That couldn't be the reason, could it? She dug deeper. "Brett and I would represent the school."

"So, it's more like a political thing?"

"Yeah," Frankie said. That sounded right.

Viveka considered this for a minute. "I thought you were over politics and just into having fun."

"I was," Frankie said, pulling the covers higher. "I didn't think it would be this much work."

The Glitterati were sleeping now, curled up and breathing deeply. The glitter on their backs glinted from the light in the hallway.

"You've stood up for causes plenty of times. You know how much work that can be."

"Yeah." Frankie turned away. "But that didn't feel like work."

"It never does when it's something you believe in," her mother said. She punctuated Frankie's forehead with a kiss. She had made her point. The end.

Frankie wanted to explain that she did believe in what she was doing. That winning was the only hard part. That the fun would kick in after that. That being the T'eau Dally High couple would mean photo shoots with Brett. Access to designer shoes and clothes. Inevitable discounts at the mall. More followers on Twitter. Limitless popularity...But how did you explain all that to a science professor? Instead, Frankie kissed her mother back and curled into fetal.

She drifted to sleep soothed by the memory of Cleo's response to her charging station. The Nile-long line had made the royal gasp; the audible suction had the force of a Dyson vacuum cleaner. Any stronger and her pita chips would have risen off their plate and stuck to her lip gloss. Haylee, on the other hand, said nothing. She simply dropped her basket of individually wrapped "Oat for Me" bars and stared.

Whoever said success is sweet was wrong. It's mint.

FRIDAY, JUNE 17
"Ahhhhhhhhhhhhhh!" cried Grace Collard.

Marc Beane kept stabbing her in the chest. The Canon stalked him like the barrel of a sniper's rifle. But he blocked it out. Being shot was the least of Marc's concerns. He'd come for blood. "The redder, the better, the deader," he shouted over Grace's shrieks.

The eye on the Canon was fixed on her now. "Help me!" she cried.

"And…cut!" Brett called from behind the lens. The audience burst into applause.

"That was killer!" panted Marc, admiring the haunted-castle backdrop, which was now splattered with red syrup.

"You know, you guys can hang out in my horror-movie shed anytime you want. I have all the *Scream*s." Brett leaned closer to Marc and winked. "You can snuggle during the scary parts."

Frankie giggled as she offered a pair of authentic bolt earrings to Grace as a parting gift.

"These are so wattage!" The girl shrieked all over again.

Wattage? How voltage!

Sorting bolts, Frankie peered across the cafeteria, evaluating her competition. Cleo was hard at work "Binding Binders"—a fancy way of saying wrapping school supplies in linen. Deuce was by her side winning the hearts and votes of practical jokers by taking off his glasses and turning unsuspecting victims' homework to stone. Haylee was set up over by the cheerleaders' table, offering free tutoring and essay revision while Heath chugged soda and burped fire on request.

Someone tapped Frankie on the shoulder. "Make me an ace belly bolt, willya?" asked Blue with a bubbly smile. The linen-wrapped bottle of hand cream poking out of her canvas tote tugged at Frankie's heart space. *Whose side is she on?*

"Aww, come on, Sheila, don't be cross," Blue said, her eyes beaming sincerity. "We're all cobbers here. I can't choose. Besides, only a square takes sides, right?"

Frankie considered this and then grinned. "And only a star

106

would see your point," she said, offering up the shiny peg and her brightest smile.

"Bonzer!" said Blue, twisting it into her belly button.

"Next!"

"I'll have what m'lass just had," said Irish Emmy.

For the next forty-three minutes, Frankie attached her father's spare bolts to fingernails, earlobes, necks, noses, wrists, and an invisible forehead (Billy's!). The line in front of her table was longer than Cleo's and Haylee's combined. And Brett was cranking out movies faster than Jennifer Aniston. Their approval rating was in the Obama-got-Osama range. Everything was positively wattage!

And then the bolts ran out.

"Quick," Brett said, handing Frankie his camera. "I need a charge."

Drained from the day before, Frankie's electric current flowed like expired OPI. Thick and slow, sticky and clumpy, the reboot was taking forever.

"Bolts are for dolts! Horror is a snorer!" Cleo called. "Come and design your own jewelry!"

Deuce was standing behind a table filled with scissors, paper scraps, and dozens of nail polish bottles. Voters were invited to cut their own shapes, and then Deuce would turn them into stone charms. If they wanted something more vibrant than the rock's natural gray color, they were invited to polish their creation with Chanel's latest summer palette. Deuce and Cleo were surrounded. All that remained in the Stein-Redding corner were syrup-stained masks, a semicharged camera, an empty box, and defeat. The crowd had definitely bolted.

Brett began packing up. Frankie began picking her seams. So what if her body fell apart? Her heart space was already broken—

"Stop it!" said a floating forehead bolt. Billy.

"Stop what?" asked Frankie, voice pinched, shoulders slumped.

"Stop telling yourself this was a big waste of time. Or that you don't stand a chance. Or that you're going to give up and go shopping . . . again!"

Frankie couldn't help grinning. He had her pegged like a pup tent.

"I really wanted to win this." *I'm so tired of failing.*

"It's not over yet," he said.

Frankie glanced at the fandemonium surrounding Cleo and Deuce. "Sure looks like it."

"Looks can be deceiving," he said. And then—*hissssssss*—Billy sprayed his face with Spectra's citrus-scented visibility mist. The bolt was stuck to the tip of his nose, not his forehead. "See?"

Frankie giggled.

"Cleo may be binding, but you've got this thing wrapped."

"How can you be so sure?" she asked.

"I just nose it," Billy said, and then began to fade. Hope, however, lingered with Frankie for the rest of the day.

TO: Jackson
June 16, 6:07 PM
MELODY: GUESS WHAT?

TO: Melody
June 16, 6:07 PM
JACKSON: CHICKEN BUTT?

TO: Jackson
June 16, 6:08 PM
MELODY: U R SUCH A DORK!

TO: Melody
June 16, 6:09 PM
JACKSON: U KNOW U LOVE IT. WHAT'S UP?

TO: Jackson
June 16, 6:10 PM
MELODY: SAGE JUST CALLED. U R NOW TEXTING THE OFFICIAL LEAD SINGER OF GRUNGE GODDESS!!!!!!!!!!!

TO: Melody
June 16, 6:12 PM
JACKSON: I KNEW YOU'D GET IT!!!

TO: Jackson
June 16, 6:12 PM
MELODY: FIRST GIG 2MORROW NITE.

TO: Melody
June 16, 6:13 PM
JACKSON: AFTER THE RAD MTG?

TO: Jackson
June 16, 6:14 PM
MELODY: CRAP. TOTALLY FORGOT. WHAT TIME IS IT?

TO: Melody
June 16, 6:14 PM
JACKSON: 7 P

TO: Jackson
June 16, 6:15 PM
MELODY: SOUND CHECK AT 6:30. I'LL TRY TO POP BY AFTER.

TO: Melody
June 16, 6:16 PM
JACKSON: TRY? POP? U HAVE TO! MR. D CALLED IT.

TO: Jackson
June 16, 6:17 PM
MELODY: K.

TO: Melody
June 16, 6:17 PM
JACKSON: PROMISE?

TO: Jackson
June 16, 6:18 PM
MELODY: YUP. THEN MY SHOW AFTER?

TO: Melody
June 16, 6:18 PM
JACKSON: PROMISE.

CHAPTER TWELVE
FRIDAY NIGHT FIGHTS

The last rays of sunshine disappeared behind the maples, and the clearing was left in the dark, just like the RADs who waited for Mr. D to make his announcement. Tall and silent as the trees that surrounded them, they stood united in their commitment to weather the storms that—

Smack!

Lala flattened a mosquito against Clawd's cheek. "No one bites my guy but me," she said, gnashing her fangs playfully. She flicked the poor-man's bloodsucker to the ground with an accomplished grin.

"Thanks," Clawd mumbled, "but that biter's the least of my worries."

"I know." Lala sighed, releasing her happy-girl act into the crisp night air. The truth was, she hated how stressed everyone was. Double hated that her father was the reason for it. And triple hated that she was just as clueless as they were. Lala shivered. Would it have killed her father to meet at RIP? Or had he not noticed that his daughter was heat-challenged? Did he even know he had a daughter?

Clawdeen linked her arm through Lala's pink peacoat. She smelled like blackberries. "Still can't say, huh?"

Lala zipped her chattering lips and turned away.

It had been h-e-double-l acting as if she were in the know. But what choice did she have? He was always locked in his office, talking in his headset, or tanning.

Brrrrap.

Heath burped a fireball and everyone gathered around. Not as much for the heat as the distraction. One by one, parents and friends stole glances at Lala, eyebrows raised with curiosity, hoping for some sort of hint. She responded with pursed lips and a shrug. . . . *I would if I could.* Blue stayed off to the side, struggling to access her Cleo-wrapped moisturizer. Her scales were starting to crack. Lala knew how they felt.

Where is he?

Jackson tapped Lala on the shoulder. His eyes were hidden behind the flames reflected in his glasses. "Do you know—?"

"I can't talk about it, okay!"

Jackson took a defensive step back. "Fine, I'll ask someone else."

"Ask me," Spectra said from somewhere nearby. "I know everything."

He hesitated for a second and then sighed in a nothing-to-lose sort of way. "Do you know where Melody is?"

Oops.

"Sure do," said the violet-scented voice. "I heard she got grounded for trashing her father's motorcycle."

112

Jackson scoffed. "Her father doesn't have a motorcycle."

"Not anymore," Spectra said. "That's why he's so mad. He loved that thing more than he loved his own son."

"He doesn't have a—" Jackson paused. "Forget it."

A sudden breeze sent the fire dancing. Maddy Gorgon quickly turned it to stone before its embers spread. Everything felt cold again. Darkness had returned. Everyone was still.

Then the sound of crunching leaves, slow and measured, grew closer.

The superior had arrived.

Lala's heart began to speed. Clawd, sensing her anxiety (or maybe his own), allowed his arm to graze hers in public. An owl hooted. Ghoulia groaned.

"The time is nigh..."—from somewhere in the tall shadows, Mr. D's voice was low and controlled, his Eastern European accent a melodic embellishment—"...to take the final step toward securing our bloodlines."

He stepped into the moonlight. Hands at his sides, shoulders back, black eyes shifting from one face to the next, Mr. D appeared before his people with the stateliness of a king. If Lala hadn't felt so dejected, she might have been proud.

"As many of our elders know, we are standing on sacred ground...."

Sacred? Does he mean scared? *Is this a language-barrier thing?*

Just as confused, Lala's friends exchanged glances.

"It was in this clearing, seventy normie years ago, that we gathered to seek refuge from our enemies. Afraid to show our faces, we dug caverns and went underground, literally. Our first tombs, coffins, labs, caves...they're all beneath us, and thanks to these changing times, they are behind us."

"Awoooooooooo!" howled the Wolfs. Others applauded. Clawdeen curtsied.

Mr. D held up a pale palm. The clearing fell silent. "Normies and RADs are now living in harmony. Some are even dating."

More applause. Frankie and Heath smiled proudly. Mr. D's palm silenced them again.

"Toleration is sublime. But integration? Assimilation? Those can be toxic. Allow them to enter our systems, and they will corrupt our DNA, weaken our bloodlines, annihilate the very things that make us special...that make us RADs...that make us superior."

Superior?

Ghoulia groaned again.

"Now that we are free, we can launch new agendas! Teach our ways! Harness our powers! Propagate the race!"

"Seems like the whole congratulations thing was a bit of a porky pie," Blue whispered.

If that meant it was a long shot, Lala couldn't have agreed more.

Mr. D snapped his fingers. Muscles appeared by his side with a gold-plated shovel. The superior thanked his aide with a dismissive nod and lifted the shovel high. "Which is why, with the help of Ram de Nile and Wolf Construction, I have purchased this land so I may bring you, and all future RAD generations, Radcliffe High!" He jammed the shovel into the loamy earth and scooped up a pile of dirt. "Construction has officially begun!"

Many of the parents cheered. Most of the kids didn't. Instead, they turned to Lala, as if she might be able to make sense of her father's bewildering announcement.

"Why didn't my dad tell me about this?" Clawd mumbled.

Blue arched her brows in an *Is this fair dinkum?* sort of way.

I seriously cannot believe you kept this from me, Cleo said with a single squint.

Your father knew about it. He bought the land. Blame him! Lala thought as she glared at Ram de Nile.

I seriously cannot believe you kept this from me and Cleo, the spiked fur on the back of Clawdeen's neck seemed to say.

Your father knew about it. He's in charge of construction. Blame him! Lala thought as she glared at Clawrk Wolf.

Is Clawd touching your arm in public? Ghoulia managed to ask with a simple smirk.

Yes, Ghouls, he's touching my arm in public. And that's about all I know, Lala conveyed with a nod.

"Say good-bye to Merston High," Mr. D said. "Starting this September, you will be attending the first RAD-only private school."

Frankie tugged her seams.

Heath popped a Tums.

Jackson hand-fanned his face while searching the clearing for someone—probably Melody.

"Sounds like someone had a fight with Majorca," Spectra told Billy.

Clawd sighed. "Looks like I'll be working construction all summer."

Mr. D went on to explain that the facility would be state-of-the-art. That classes and sports would cater to the RADs' individual skills and needs. That this school would be a destination for RADs from all over the world—several had already enrolled, and some had already arrived in Salem. But all Lala could think about was the T'eau Dally contest. What was she supposed to do now? Forfeit?

"Any questions?" Mr. D asked.

Hands shot up.

"What about Double RAmies?" Frankie asked. "This separation could do some serious damage to the relationships."

Heath nodded in agreement.

"You're not leaving town. Just switching schools."

"What if I still want to play football for Merston?" (Clawd.)

"Radcliffe needs you, son. You play for us now."

"And basketball?" (Deuce.)

"We will have our own basketball team too."

"Can we still compete against normie schools?" (Clawdeen.)

"If they are brave enough to welcome our superior teams into their leagues."

"What happens to my swim scholarship?" (Blue.)

"And my track scholarship?" (Rocks.)

"Scholarships will no longer be necessary. We are currently developing a RAD college. Standards will be high, but tuition will be low."

Several of the parents applauded.

"We tried so hard to fit in with the normies. This feels like a step backward." (Clawdeen.)

Mr. D forced a patient smile. "You'll still have time to socialize with the…others. Just not on school days or at weekend sporting events."

Frankie sparked. "Do we have a choice?"

"I'd rather stay."

"Me too."

"Same."

Mr. D's expression hardened. A cold breeze blew. His hair did not. "Attendance at Radcliffe High is mandatory for all RADs."

A collective gasp rattled the branches above.

"Meeting adjourned."

"What about all the normies who worship me?" Cleo whispered to Lala. "They'll be lost. And what about the contest? Me and Deuce are about to become spokesmodels. You have to do something!"

Lala knew Cleo was right. But what were her options? Conversation certainly wasn't one. *Dad, can you hear me now? How about now? Now?* Their entire relationship was one massive dropped call.

"What about the contest?" Frankie called out.

"What contest?"

Dozens of eyes turned to Lala. *He doesn't know about the contest?*

Lala became light-headed. Her insides felt floaty. She was about to have a major fang-xiety attack.

"Thanks to Lala, Merston's a finalist in the T'eau Dally high school contest," Frankie explained. "If we win, we'll get to redo the whole school. And Brett and I get to—"

"Brett and I?" Cleo screeched. "More like Deuce and I."

"What about me and Haylee?" Heath asked. "We're in this too, you know. And we have a better chance than you because of our Double RAmie status."

117

Cleo put her hands on her hips. "That term is so—"

"Enough!" snapped Mr. D. "Whatever this little contest is about, it's best left for the normies to deal with. It's time to start focusing on your own community."

Little contest? LITTLE CONTEST?

Shaking and floaty, Lala stepped forward and blurted, "Merston *is* our community."

Mr. D slowly turned around to face his daughter. Frankie sparked but stood firmly by Lala's side.

"Not anymore," he said with an eerie sense of calm. "You have a new school. You don't need to compete for one in a sad little contest." His dark eyes gripped her like a vise. "Withdraw."

Lala shook her head. "You've been pressuring me to do something for my school all year. Now that I am, you want me to withdraw?"

"Lala!" Clawd urged. "Be careful—"

"You will do as I say."

"Why?" Lala folded her arms across her chest. "You'll just change your mind again."

There were gasps from the crowd.

Mr. D stabbed the shovel into the ground. "Draculaura, wait for me in the parlor at home. Everyone else, this meeting is adjourned."

Flames trembled in the glass-screened fireplace.

Lala sat on the edge of the daybed and rolled back her shoulders. She smoothed Count Fabulous's pink bangs, lifted her chin, and then clasped her hands for warmth. The pose reminded her of the time her grimparents had commissioned Densilav Blega to paint her portrait. Only that time she'd been shaking with boredom, not anticipation.

Before leaving the clearing, Clawd had urged Lala to apologize to her father. Blue and Clawdeen wished her luck and begged her to call them the minute she could. Frankie offered to hide her in the Fab. But Lala refused. What could he possibly do? Kill her? Been there, bit that, 1,599 years ago.

Uncle Vlad appeared by her side, smelling like eucalyptus. "Another scoop?" he asked, spoon at the ready.

Lala rubbed her belly and shook her head. She wanted her father's attention, but puking soybean pâté on his new jeans was hardly the way to get it. "Maybe some peppermint tea," she said, handing Vlad her plate.

"A little too much comfort food?"

"A little too much food," Lala said, peering out the window, "and not enough comfort."

"I wish I could have been there to—ahhh…ahhh…"—Uncle Vlad set down his serving tray, dug into the pocket of his kimono, and thrust a silk hankie toward his nose—"chehhhhh!"

"Bless you."

He reached under his glasses and dabbed the corners of his eyes. "I told him—no, I begged him—not to leave that vitamin C–sucking paper shredder in my health corner, but did he listen?" Vlad paused to blow his nose. "'Course not." He blew again. "What do I know about fang shui? I only wrote the book and created the app. Not to mention the—"

Headlights fanned across the walls in the parlor. The town car crunched across the gravel driveway.

119

"I'll be right back with your tea," Vlad said, scooting off.

The front door creaked open. In the bedroom above, her pets scurried to their hiding places. Count Fabulous, still perched on her wrist, began to quake. Lala pressed her hand against his tapping heart. She wished there were a Rosetta Stone DVD that taught animal language, so she could tell her friends to relax. Her father's bite was bad, but his bark was worse. Besides, he had no interest in them. He had no interest in anyone or anything other than his work. And yet there she was, century after century, stressing to impress.

Thwack!

Footsteps clicked against the marble floors. Clarity smacked Lala like a bat with a spastic wing. A wise old man once said, "Maybe he's just not that into you." And maybe that guy was right. So why not speak her mind? At this point, winning was the only thing left to lose.

Count Fabulous flapped away, his pink bang extensions falling to the rug. Lala leaned forward to get them but met with the shiny tip of her father's shoe instead. He ground the bat bangs like a lit cigarette. *What an ash!*

"How dare you defy me," he said, glaring down at her.

At least he was there, not in HD but three-D. Breathing the same firewood-scented air she was. It was the first time they had communicated in the parlor without a flat screen. The realization made her grin. And that made him batty.

"I am the superior!" he insisted, fangs bared. "When I tell you to do something, you are expected to do it. I am also your father—"

Ha!

"By bite," she managed to mutter, "not blood."

A gasp came from the hallway. It was followed by a sneeze.

Vlad had been eavesdropping. But neither Mr. D nor Lala seemed to care. Instead, they stood frozen, her claim whipping around the room like an icy wind.

A memory of searing hunger. A damp chill. Of being carried through snow...red droplets falling, marking a trail. Each chest-shattering cough reverberating though her body...spouting more blood...mounting a staircase...It was warmer now. The silver light of the moon was gone. Warm orange flickers guided them. She was placed on a bed. It smelled of coins and salty skin. The sheets, once satiny and smooth, were soaked in perspiration. Her mother moaning beside her, asking to see Laura....*I'm here, Mama*, she wanted to say, but it was too hard to speak....Mr. D insisting Laura was right there....Bone-aching exhaustion...hearing her mother's final gasp for air...silently begging her not to go...Mr. D racing into the room...calling her mother's name... *Alina...Alina...Alina*...pulling her to him, as if she was more than just his housekeeper...as if he was less than Romanian royalty. A doctor announcing it was too late...Mr. D's shoulders shaking...saying he wished he could have saved her, wished the snow hadn't kept him from her...The doctor saying the girl didn't have much longer...Mr. D leaning over her...wiping her sweat-drenched hair aside...An excruciating stab in her neck... paralyzing pressure...darkness...and then a new day. Her strength was back. Her mother was gone. And for some reason, all she could think about was sinking her odd-shaped teeth into a slab of raw steak.

Lala blinked back tears. "You never should have saved me."

He poured himself a glass of five-hundred-year-old scotch.

"It's obvious you never wanted a daughter."

"Wrong!" he said, slamming his crystal glass down on the polished black side table.

"Coaster!" called Vlad.

Mr. D ignored him.

"You should have asked Mr. Stein to build you a robot. Someone who would do exactly what you wanted, exactly the way you wanted her to. Because I—"

"I don't want a robot," he interrupted. "But I also don't want an unmotivated, disrespectful fang-banger who—"

Lala stomped her foot. "Unmotivated?! Because of me, Merston is one of three finalists in the whole country! I did that, Dad, me!" Lala beat her chest like an orangutan, desperate for him to see her. "And what's a fang-banger? Is that even a thing?"

He lifted the glass to his lips and took a small sip of the amber liquid. "Radcliffe High will be good for you."

Lala twisted her hair around her finger and tugged. "How do you know what's good for me? You're never even here! And when you are, it's like you're not—only worse, because you are, but you're ignoring me." Hearing those words aloud sharpened their meaning and stabbed Lala in the chest. "I had no idea you were even working on this school. No idea. Do you know how pathetic that is?"

"Well, I had no idea about your little contest," he countered.

"It's not little!" Lala snapped. "It happens to be national. And I tried to tell you about it, but you wouldn't listen and—" Her throat tensed. "I *thought* you would be proud. That's the only reason I entered in the first place."

"I'll be proud when you stop wasting time with your friends and you start getting serious about—"

"My friends are my family now. And for the last year, we've worked hard to become part of this community and—" Tears began to fall. Lala hid her face. In all her 1,599 years, he had never seen her cry.

Mr. D made no effort to console her. Instead, he stood back and watched her sob. "Your friends will never save you like I saved you."

"They already have."

He sighed and then checked his pocket watch. "The point is, no one should have to save you, Laura," he said. It was the first time he'd used her real name since… "You need to be strong. Strong enough to shut out distractions and focus on what really matters."

Lala wiped her eyes with the back of her hand. The cold skin soothed her puffy lids. "Strength isn't about keeping people out." She sniffled. "It's about letting them in."

Mr. D pointed a finger at her. "You say that today. But what are you going to preach tomorrow? Or the next day? One minute it's health food and animal makeovers, and the next it's world peace!"

He'd noticed!

"You never follow through on anything. That's why your cousins call you Count Slackula!"

They do?

Vlad snorted.

"It's not funny!" she called.

Mr. D's phone rang. He checked the screen and then answered.

"Hold the line," he told the caller. He turned back to his daughter. "I'll make you a deal."

Lala raised an eyebrow at him.

"I'm not raising you to be a quitter. So finish this little contest. When you lose, you'll leave Merston and go to Radcliffe."

"And if I win?"

Mr. D lifted an eyebrow.

"If I win?"

He covered the mouthpiece of his phone. "You stay."

Hmmm. Not bad for a fang-banger.

LOST CHAPTER

(WHOSE UNLUCKY NUMBER SHALL GO UNMENTIONED)

CHAPTER FOURTEEN
BIRDS OF A FEATHER

No longer home to a paper factory, the warehouse had been magically transformed into a sold-out performance venue. Amid blinding red lights, whistle-laced applause, and a mass of unfamiliar faces, Melody followed her bandmates onto the boot-scuffed stage.

Cici strapped a silver bass over her CHICKS WITH PICKS tee. Sage lifted her doodle-covered guitar. Nine-Point-Five raised her nail polish–painted sticks toward the tin ceiling. Her Pikachu tank slipped up, and her belly roll plopped down. The audience applauded.

Melody stepped toward the mike. Grabbed it by its cold steely stem. Looked down at her pink Converse. Licked her dry lips. Searched for the nearest exit.

It was too late to run. Instead, she had to quiet her mind. But how? It felt as though it had been plugged into Sage's amp. The Goddesses had taken turns consoling her. Reminding her that these things happen. That no matter what goes down, they have each other now. But nothing changed the fact that the sound check had run long. That she had chosen the band over the RAD meeting. That she had broken a promise to Jackson. That she wished she were sorry but she wasn't. That—

"One, two, three, four!" Nine-Point-Five beat the opening of Fiona Apple's "Sleep to Dream." The others joined in. Melody closed her eyes. She began to sing. Everything but the music fell away.

Luscious Jackson, Soundgarden, and even Britney (tweaked until cool, of course). Nothing but blink-fast images remained. Sweat-soaked girls waving their arms in the air...college guys gazing at her...others singing along...cell phone flames held high...Candace and Spectra blowing her kisses...Candace on Billy's shoulders...people freaking because she appeared to be levitating...Jackson off to the side with his hand fan...happy that he came.

But most of what Melody experienced during the fifty-five-minute set was a feeling. Floating? Flying? No. It was more like soaring. Like the old warehouse, she, too, had been magically transformed.

The show was over and the spell had been broken. DJ Gold Chedda began blasting Pitbull for the late-night crowd—aka, those too cheap to pay a live-music cover. And Melody was back to being just another girl trying to make things right with her boyfriend.

Crossing the obstacle-ridden dance floor felt more like being a contestant on *Wipeout*. And then she spotted Jackson by the Monster Energy drink bar.

"Jackson!"

"Hey!" A flamboyant guy grabbed her by the shoulders and spun her around. "Don't be yelling and ruining that voice, girl." His clammy hand soaked through her breath-strip-thin black tee. Candace had paid $175 for the hole-filled rag. But since it looked as if it had been pulled off a hitchhiker, Melody had agreed to wear it. Now, thanks to the Clam Man, it smelled hitchhiker-y too. "Your voice is the atom!"

Melody backed away.

"You know, the bomb?"

"Thanks," she said politely. "I-I just have to find someone, so . . ."

"No worries," he said, applauding as she wiggled deeper into the dancing crowd.

"Your voice is sick!" cried a girl as a boy was grinding against her thigh.

"Love the feathers!" called out another girl, mid-twirl.

"Biggest fan!" yelled a shirtless male with a tattoo of Gwen Stefani on his chest.

"Join us." A girl with white-blond hair and short bangs grabbed Melody by the wrist and pulled her into the rump-shaking circle. Hands above her head, she gave herself into the music, surrendering to the strobing lights and the crush of bodies for a full minute before tearing herself away. *Jackson first, euphoria later.*

Melody, caught between two full-bottomed girls in fishnets and short shorts, was bumped forward like a pinball. She crashed

128

into a guy wearing dog tags and a white tank. He pulled her toward his nautical-scented chest and began swiveling his hips as if riding the open seas.

"Awww, come awn!" Melody winced, shoving him away. But he refused to let her go.

"Come on, sing for me."

"Ew!" she said, struggling to free her wrist. His grip was strong but effortless, as if he were holding a string of helium balloons bobbing in the breeze.

Melody began to panic. She searched the crowd for a familiar face and finally saw Jackson. He was standing off to the side of the floor, shifting from side to side, clenching his fists in frustration while she struggled. She shot him a *Save me!* glare. He waved his hand fan. Short for *I would if I could but I'll sweat so I won't*. Instead, he tapped his fingers against his thumb as if working a hand puppet and signaled her to use her voice.

Oh yeah!

Just as Melody was about to tell the fiend Marine to go pee his pants and then run home sucking his thumb, someone lifted her up and ran her off the dance floor. His body was stone-cold and solid. If Jackson was an *udon* noodle, this guy was manicotti— al dente.

He placed her down gently by the Monster Energy drink bar. "Hi, I'm G—"

"Thanks, man," Jackson said, wrapping a protective arm around Melody. "I can take it from here."

Before she had a chance to thank the stranger or even get a decent look at him, Jackson had led her into a dark corner. "You okay?"

Melody nodded, reaching for his bottle of water.

"What happened to you tonight?" he asked, hazel eyes wide with concern. "You said you were going to be at the meeting and—"

"Sound check ran long," Melody said, straining to spot her mysterious savior amid the flashing lights and shifting bodies. "I'm sorry. I should have called, but…"

"The show was great," he said with a sincere smile. "You were great."

"I was?" Melody asked, surprised. *He's not mad?*

"Better than great. You should have heard what people were saying about you." The concern in his eyes morphed into pride. *He's not mad!*

Melody lifted herself onto her toes and kissed his soft lips. An apology for underestimating his coolness. And another for showing up in her favorite denim jacket, even though it was hot in there.

"So." Jackson quickly pulled away. "I've got some great news."

"What?" Melody asked, arms still clasped behind his back.

"I was going to tell you at the meeting, but—"

"Melly!" Sage called.

Melody giggled as the guitarist danced toward her. As usual, Sage looked like a *Teen Vogue* version of rock. Thick black hair, dark red lipstick, ironic T-shirt, ironic tutu, and motorcycle boots. Her dark eyes and cocoa-colored Neutrogena skin reminded Melody of a chocolate-covered almond: smooth and impossible to resist. She was too pretty for rock, too cool for pop. And she was calling Melody's name!

Melody turned away from Jackson and signaled for Sage to come over.

Jackson broke free of Melody's grip.

"What?"

"I was about to tell you."

Melody giggled at her thoughtlessness. "Omigod, I'm so sorry, you're right. What is it?"

Jackson's face illuminated. "We got them!"

Them? "You mean the leather bracelets we ordered?"

Jackson shook his head. "The jobs."

Jobs?

"At Camp Crescendo. We got them!"

Melody's thoughts shifted and locked. *Oh yeah, camp.* "That's great!" she said.

He leaned down and kissed her sweetly. "Think about it. Two months, just you and me. Camping, singing, painting—"

Sage slung her arms around Melody and squeezed.

"You bolted so fast that we never got to tell you what an awesome gig that was," Sage yelled into her ear. Then she greeted Jackson with a fist bump. "Cici and Nine are backstage looking for you."

"Sorry, I just wanted to find Jackson before—"

"This is Granite," Sage announced.

A boy—the boy—in the leather jacket leaned forward, flashed the side of his hand, and leaned back. Something zapped Melody's insides. It felt like she'd run into an electric fence.

"He's our roadie," Sage chirped. "And our eye candy," she teased, mussing his black Dave Navarro–style ponytail. But it was obvious she wasn't kidding. Along with his al dente body,

131

Granite's narrow eyes—an unusually light shade of gray—gripped Melody like magnets.

"Thanks for saving me from that freak out there," she managed.

He shrugged as though it was no big deal. "You looked like you were in trouble, so..."

Jackson cleared his throat. "Mel, it's getting hot in here. We should probably get going."

She nodded. "Sure." And then to Granite, "So, uh, thanks for packing up our stuff and everything."

"Mel, we should really get going."

"Going?" Sage interrupted. "The DJ just started."

"It's a different D.J. that concerns me," Jackson said, reaching for Melody's hand. She wanted to go with him. The last thing she needed was D.J. Hyde swooping in, telling everyone how much he hated girl bands and ruining the perfect night. But for some reason she couldn't move.

All of a sudden Cici and Nine appeared, flushed and panting.

"I just requested Björk," Cici announced.

"'Human Behaviour'?" Melody asked, hoping.

Nine nodded. "Club remix."

On cue, heavy industrial beats began pumping all around them. The red lights turned to steely blue. Faux fog hissed down from above. Cici and Nine yanked Melody, Sage, and Granite onto the dance floor. Melody looked back at Jackson like a helpless kidnapping victim. "Go without me," she called through the smoke. "I'll get a ride home with Candace."

He flashed her a thumbs-up and raced for the exit.

Oops. Siren alert! Did I just use my voice on Jackson?

Melody turned to her new friends and banged her head, shaking out her guilt with each cranial thrust. Accidents do happen.

The house lights came on like a slap. *Wake up! Party's over! Time to get your sweaty butts to bed*, they seemed to say.

"Already?" Nine whined.

Cici checked her armful of Swatches. "It's one o'clock."

The girls giggled, marveling at their stamina. Only a handful of people remained, most of whom were staff, none of whom was Candace.

"Van's loaded," Granite said, dropping a set of keys into Sage's hand.

"Mind if I catch a ride?" Melody asked.

"If you don't mind sitting on Nine-Point-Five's lap," Sage said.

Nine gripped her roll of belly fat. "It comes complete with air bags."

"Or would you prefer saddlebags?" Cici said, slapping her meaty outer thighs.

"I like it all," Melody said, wondering what her parents would think of her rolling up after midnight stuffed in a van.

"How about I take you?" Granite offered.

"I guess it would be safer that way," she rationalized, ignoring the scratched motorcycle helmet tucked under his arm, the teeming rain echoing off the tin roof, and the fact that she was required to wrap her arms around his stone-cold body while riding—the last of which was safe in a dangerous sort of way.

They stepped into the bone-chilling night. Other than the

occasional *whoosh* of a passing car, the dilapidated block was silent. Rain fell sideways all around them and stung Melody's bare arms.

"You don't happen to have an umbrella, do you?" Granite asked.

Melody giggled. "You afraid of a little water?" she teased.

"Nah," he said, lifting his palm above his head. Water trickled down the backs of his fingers as if they were drainpipes. "I was worried about your feathers."

"Oh," Melody said, examining his dry clothes. "They're um, they…It's okay. Birds get wet all the time. So…how are you doing that?"

He placed the helmet on her head and lifted his other hand. The water stopped falling on her too.

"Have you ever been on a bike before?" he asked, straddling his black-and-silver motorcycle. He took off his jacket and draped it over her narrow shoulders.

Melody nodded, even though she hadn't. Something in her wanted him to think she was just as cool as he was. But why? He didn't seem to care about cool.

Granite stepped on the clutch, and the engine sparked to life.

"Aren't you going to wear a helmet?" she asked.

"Nah. My head is like a rock," he said. "Hold on tight."

Melody wrapped her arms around his worn white T-shirt. It felt like hugging a statue.

They zipped down the slick road amid streetlights reflecting halos—a black-and-white photograph come to life.

"How was that?" Granite asked, pulling up in front of Melody's house.

Over too fast.

134

"Great," she said, removing the helmet and handing it to him. The rain had slowed to a drizzle. "Thanks again for—"

Ping! Ping! Their phones signaled text messages at the exact same time.

"Probably your boyfriend," he said.

And your girlfriend? she might have asked. If she cared. Which she didn't.

They checked their screens, and Melody read her message:

TO: Melody
June 18, 1:22 AM
MR. D: RAD MEETINGS ARE MANDATORY. ROCK CONCERTS ARE NOT.

"Whatever," Granite muttered under his breath.

Melody stiffened. Hand umbrella, stone-cold body, clear gray eyes... "What are you?"

"Huh?" He slipped his phone in the back pocket of his jeans.

"That text. It was the same as mine, wasn't it?"

"Depends," he said, his gray eyes fixed on hers. "What did yours say?"

"Something about rock concerts."

"No way," Granite said calmly, incapable of losing his cool.

"Yes, way!" Melody said, cool lost. "We're both RADs!"

"I knew there was something different about you," he said. "So, what are you? Some kind of Siren?"

Melody nodded. "Impressive. What are you? Some kind of umbrella?"

"Close," he snickered. "I'm a gargoyle. Put on old buildings to keep the rain from dripping down the sides and eroding them."

"And to freak people out," Melody teased.

He snickered again. "That too."

"So where do you...live?"

"I did live in Portland. Right over the entrance of Venue, the oldest rock bar in the country. Every cool act came through there. It was incredible, until they demolished it last month."

"Starbucks?"

"Coffee Bean."

"Sucks." Melody sighed.

"Big-time. My parents sent me here because the school here is"—he made air quotes—"'RAD-friendly.' But I think I'm going to stick with the music thing. Life experience will teach me more than sitting in some classroom."

The porch lights flicked on. Slapped again.

"I'd better go," Melody said, not moving.

He took out his phone and bumped her his number. "In case you need your microphone packed up."

"Thanks." She smiled. There was nothing wrong with making a new friend, was there?

She turned as Granite's taillight faded down the street, and caught a glimpse of Jackson looking out his bedroom window. She blew him a kiss. But his curtains swung shut before he caught it. The kiss dwindled in the breeze, fading like the smoke of a doused flame.

CHAPTER FIFTEEN
GREEN PLEAS

Principal Weeks leaned across the podium and turtled his neck toward the microphone. "Testing...testing." His usual drill was to demand silence, but the minute he took the stage, the chatter stopped. Today, no one wanted to miss a word.

Frankie turned in her front-row seat and smiled politely at her competitors. But Cleo and Haylee were too busy swapping a secret to notice. Their close-talking camaraderie struck Frankie as odd, considering the golden girl and the brownnoser were about as tight as a boyfriend sweater. Maybe their dads had lectured them about good sportsmanship too.

"Nervous?" Brett whispered into Frankie's ear.

"No," she said, smoothing her black-and-white-striped hair. How could anyone be nervous in a glitter-speckled minidress, new plaid booties, and lips slathered in MAC's Viva Glam Gaga gloss? If looks could kill, she'd be serving back-to-back life sentences. "Why? Do I look nervous?"

"You look like a winner," Brett said, and then gently kissed her neck bolt.

Frankie sparked. "Are you sure you don't want to be part of my presentation?"

"Stage fright," he reminded her.

She giggled. There was something about a horror-film fanatic with stage fright that Frankie found charmingly mint. Of all the things to be afraid of!

"Hello, Merston!" Principal Weeks bellowed. "We're here to choose a couple to represent our school—and hopefully the T'eau Dally brand—for the next year." Applause erupted behind the candidates' VIP seats. Frankie and Brett squeezed each other's hands. Haylee bit her bottom lip. Cleo and Deuce high-fived.

"Go, Frankieeee!" shouted a girl from the back.

Frankie turned, smiled graciously, and then crossed her green legs.

Cleo and Haylee exchanged a loaded glance. Frankie wanted to lean over and tell them not to be jealous. That it all boiled down to the speeches. That they still had a chance. But Principal Weeks was holding up his palm, insisting on silence, and she didn't dare disobey. She wanted his vote.

"As you know," he continued, "winning this contest would mean national recognition for Merston High. Not to mention one million dollars in upgrades—"

Applause rolled through the auditorium.

"—which I am hoping will be enough to keep the RADs from leaving to attend Radcliffe High."

Clawd cupped his hands over his mouth. "Boooooo!"

Lala buried her face against his arm. *Poor vamp*, thought Frankie. Winning this sponsorship suddenly meant more than prize money and national fame. Because of the deal Lala had made with her father, winning meant keeping RADs and normies together at Merston. Losing meant the end of everything they had been fighting for. Frankie began tugging her wrist seams, suddenly feeling the pressure. Were she and Brett the best people for that job? Cleo and Deuce were Merston royalty. Haylee and Heath were both prized students. Being voted the It Couple was only a minor success. The real victory would come after they won over the sponsors. *If* they won over the sponsors...

What if she got voted in and the T'eau Dally people didn't like her? Then whose fault would it be if they had to switch schools? Frankie sparked.

"No more RADs at Merston would mean the end of our championship sports teams, and a significant cut in state funding." More boos.

In a show of empathy, Frankie reached behind Brett and placed her arm on the metal back of Lala's chair. "No one blames you," she whispered.

Lala nodded appreciatively until her black hair began to rise. Strand by strand, it floated to the top of her head until it resembled Clawd's mohawk.

"Frankie!" she hissed.

Principal Weeks glared at them.

"Whoops!" Frankie pulled her arm off the chair. The static electricity faded, and Lala's hair returned to its normal glossy state.

"Before we get too down in the dumps, I'd like to introduce

139

the student who single-handedly brought T'eau Dally to Merston. The girl on whom our hope now rests: Lala!" Principal Weeks gestured grandly while everyone cheered.

Lala's fully exposed fangs symbolized her newfound pride as she stepped up to the podium. "Hey," she said shyly. Her voice was aftershock shaky, but she stood up straight and looked directly at the crowd. "In three days, Brigitte T'eau and Dickie Dally—"

"She said Dickie!" someone whispered.

Lala busted out laughing along with everyone else. Principal Weeks scanned the rows.

"Continue, please," he said.

"Our job is to pick the couple the T'eau Dally representatives will like best, not the ones we like best, so vote with your heads, not with your hearts. The future of RADs at Merston depends on it. So let's get started with Frankie Stein and Brett Redding!" Lala stepped off to the side like a presenter at the Oscars.

Mindful of not slipping or sparking, Frankie blocked out the cheers and recited the alphabet while mounting the stage—a relaxation technique her mother had picked up during her early days of teaching.

By the time Frankie got to *T*, she was all set up at the podium. No slips, no sparks. Just an auditorium full of expectant faces, eager to judge.

Yellow bolts crackled from her fingertips. "Ooops. Sorry!" She giggled. *Start confident*. "Hi. I'm, um, Frankie. And my boyfriend, Brett, and I are the best couple to represent Merston in the T'eau Dally contest because, like the shoes, we are two different things that have come together as one. For starters, he's got stage fright and I don't." She giggled again. The expectant faces didn't even crack a smile. "But, um, more importantly"—she sparked again—"he's a normie. I'm, obviously, a RAD, as you can see by the sparks that are melting my manicure." More silence. "And speaking of electricity, uh, he has bolts and I have nuts—"

Laughter.

Brett buried his face in his hands.

"Wait, I mean, I have bolts and he has nuts! Wait, no ..." Murmurs and snickers built all around her. She was losing them. Even Principal Weeks was checking his BlackBerry. "And that's kind of how Brett and I are...." Frankie's heart space seized. Her gut space churned. Her brain space asked for one more chance. "Because we're so different, we're kind of like a male and female socket, you know? How one goes into the other?"

"Yeah, baby!" hooted Candace Carver.

"Wooo-hooo," echoed Candace's friends.

Blue and Clawdeen buried their faces in their hands.

Frankie abandoned her notes. "Basically, you guys know me, right? And you know Brett." Scattered applause. "You know we're super fun. We're super nice. And we're obviously super stylish." She twirled in her glitter dress. Her supporters *woot-woot*ed. Voltage! She was winning them back. "And if you vote for us, we promise to show T'eau Dally that we are just as perfectly mismatched as their sneakers and pumps. If we were food, we'd be a Big Mac and a Diet Coke. A spring trend? We'd be florals and plaids. A haircut? We'd be a mullet. A—"

Bzzzzzzz.

Lala approached the podium and hip-nudged Frankie aside. "Time's up. Thank you very much, Frankie and Brett."

"Woooo-hoooooo!" Billy and Spectra shouted from somewhere.

Others eventually joined in, until the applause had spread like a current. Frankie grinned and curtsied.

"Up next, Haylee and Heath," Lala announced.

Cleo and Deuce approached the podium. Her three-inch T'eau heels clomped across the plywood. Deuce's Dally high-tops squeaked dutifully behind. *Nice touch.*

Lala looked just as confused as everyone else, and Haylee just pushed her beige glasses up her oily T-zone and slumped down in her seat.

Cleo unhooked the microphone as if she were on the last stop of her worldwide tour. "Unfortunately, Heath and Haylee are out of the race. They thank you for considering them and ask that you respect their privacy during this time."

Several students in the second row leaned forward to ask the couple if Cleo's announcement was true. Frankie glanced at Haylee, who mouthed back, *I'm sorry.* Sorry for what? Heath simply looked at Brett and shrugged as though he had no idea what was going on, nor did he care.

"What part of 'respect their privacy' don't you get?" Cleo snapped.

The first two rows faced forward, and the murmurs stopped. *Why would Haylee quit? And why did she confide in Cleo? No offense, Glitterati, but I smell a rat.*

Cleo banged her yellow stack of index cards on the podium and rolled back her bronzed shoulders.

"Index cards?" Billy whispered as he sat on the floor and leaned against Frankie's legs.

"I heard she hired Bill Clinton's former speechwriter," Spectra added, sitting beside him.

"My name is Cleo de Nile, and I'm running with my long-term boyfriend, Deuce Gorgon." Her voice was unwavering. Her bangs glistening. Her coral dress revealing.

"And if you vote for us, we'll win for you. It's that simple. T'eau Dally is looking for a golden couple to represent the merger of function and style." She gestured to Deuce in his black beanie, white Wayfarers, and sloppy jeans. "As you can see, he's function." She gestured to the braided gold band across her black bangs. "And I'm style."

Applause.

"When it comes to high performance, well, D is the king of b-ball, and I'm queen bee." She glanced down at the cards.

Applause.

"But we're more than just great-looking faces." She paused to bat her fake lashes at Frankie. "We're environmentally best-friendly, which appeals to T'eau Dally's green ethic—"

Billy nudged Frankie on the shin. "Look," he whispered, eyeing Haylee.

Are her lips moving in time with Cleo's?

"No flyers or unrecyclable bolts in our campaign!" Cleo continued. Haylee mouthed along.

Holy shock! Cleo is reading Haylee's speech!

"And when we win, we'll take that idea even further by adding skylights to the cafeteria, solar-powered heating—"

Lala clapped. Frankie picked her seams.

"Organic food made by Harriet Wolf—"

Clawdeen and her brothers clapped.

"A spa in the nurse's office, because stress is the number one cause of illness." Haylee mouthed along.

Deuce leaned into the mike. "Video-game consoles in the locker rooms."

His teammates stood and cheered, "Deuce! Deuce! Deuce!"

Frankie picked another seam.

Cleo grabbed the mike. "Swim lanes in the halls."

"Ace!" Blue shouted.

"Rake!" called Irish Emmy.

"Solid, concrete things that T'eau Dally and Merston can be proud—"

Bzzzzzz.

Deuce leaned forward and flashed a peace sign. "Gorgon and de Nile will make you smile." He pulled Cleo in for a kiss.

"Give them a hand!" Lala shouted over roars of approval.

In a show of good sportsmanship, Frankie did. And then that hand slid off its seams and landed with a suicidal thud.

Brett quickly bent down to get it. "I don't think she was being serious."

"I don't know what to believe anymore," Frankie said, sniffling.

A gold linen strip floated down from the stage and landed on her shoulder. "Wrap it in that until you get home."

"Thanks," Frankie mumbled without looking up.

"Consider it a consolation prize," purred Cleo as three hundred–plus students lined up to vote. "Thanks for playing. It's been golden."

CHAPTER SIXTEEN
ROADIE TRIP

Melody bounded up the school steps, the soles of her Converse slapping the pavement in a loud-enough-to-get-busted sort of way. She'd skipped the assembly for a quick photo shoot with the band, and if she hurried, she could slip in unnoticed before the voting was over. At least that was what she had thought before catching a glimpse of her reflection in the glass doors: feather-fringed hair, metallic eye shadow, smudged liner, Cici's shiny gray jeggings, Sage's neon-yellow off-the-shoulder tee. She was way too Saturday night for a Monday afternoon. Principal Weeks would notice her from the NASA space shuttle. And then there was Jackson....

Melody had spent the weekend convincing him that the ride from Granite was just a ride, and they'd finally agreed not to let the band come between them. Things were back to normal. Plans for Camp Crescendo were under way...

...and then Sage had called.

New posters were their final attempt to drum up summer gigs before resorting to "real job" hunts. And attendance at the photo shoot by their new lead Goddess was mandatory. What would happen to the Camp Crescendo plan if the band got summer gigs? Melody shook the thought from her mind. She'd jump off that bridge when she came to it.

The shoot was speedy, as promised. It was just the whole *let's-rethink-the-name-of-the-band-now-that-Davina-is-gone* conversation that went into overtime. And it was still going when Melody dashed into the hallway.

STYLE DOLLS? (Cici.)

SUPERSONIC SCANDAL? (Sage.)

SONIC DIVA? (Cici.)

FOOTLOOSE AND FINGER-FREE? (Nine-Point-Five.)

ROCK GLITZ? (Sage.)

Melody's phone was *ping*ing like iTunes. She should have switched it to silent mode. Should have snapped back into school mode. Should have slipped inside the auditorium. But she couldn't move. She felt like a caged bird, wanting to fly but forced to stay grounded.

LEADFEATHER, she texted. It was the perfect way to describe the feeling.

Her bandmates responded immediately with a HELLZ YEAH!

Problem solved. No more excuses. The voting booths were waiting. What was it they were voting for, again?

Ping!

She dug for her phone. Probably Jackson wondering where she was...

146

GRANITE: OUTSIDE UR SCHOOL. MEET ME. WANNA SHOW U SOMETHING.

Another minute won't hurt. Will it?

Granite, in his usual leather jacket, worn jeans, and scuffed boots, was leaning against his motorcycle as if posing for a movie poster. His light gray eyes faced the bright sun, and yet the glare didn't seem to bother him. Nothing did.

"Hop on," he said, offering his helmet.

Melody glanced back at the mustard-colored building. Fourth period was still a half hour away. She slipped on the helmet. Like strong hands during a make-out, it gripped the sides of her face and blocked out the universe.

"Where are we going?" she asked as they merged onto I-5 north. *Definitely longer than a minute...*

Melody tried to be irritated when he didn't answer. But the sun was on her back, the wind was in her face, and Granite's abs were as taut as guitar strings. Not that Jackson's weren't. They were...just in a thinner sort of way. It was time to head back to school. To Jackson. To reality. All she had to do was lean a little closer to Granite's pointy ear and, in her best Siren voice, tell him to turn around. Instead, she held on tight and enjoyed the ride.

An hour later they were driving over a bridge that put them in downtown Portland. They zoomed past a Chinese garden, a cool record shop on Second Avenue, and tons of vintage stores that Candace would have loved. But Granite didn't slow down until they came to a squared-off pile of rubble on a busy corner of Third Avenue.

"What is this place?"

"The future site of a Coffee Bean and Tea Leaf," he said, kicking a brick.

"This was your old home?" Melody asked as the pile of rubble took on new meaning.

Granite nodded. "This was Venue." He pulled her past the caution tape and onto what used to be the beer-soaked stage. Hills of poster-covered walls lay at their feet like unwanted cookie crumbs at the bottom of the bag. He bent down and handed her a diamond-shaped rock with the word JAM on it.

"I remember when Eddie Vedder dropped off that poster," Granite said. "No one had even heard of Pearl Jam yet. He pulled his van right up to the doors and blasted the demo during a staff meeting. Vic, the owner, booked the band that night."

"Really?" Melody asked, gripping the concrete diamond as if it were the Hope.

"I dunno if it's cuz I was watching from up high or what, but that Vedder is one short dude," Granite said. He ran a finger down the cracked wood bar, raising a cloud of dust that frolicked in the sun.

"What happened to the other gargoyles?"

"The architect came by and pried them loose before the wrecking ball came. He wanted them for a bank he was designing." He paused. "I couldn't do it."

"Do what?"

He helped her over a pile of broken tables.

"Spend the next hundred years above a bank." He winced. "Could you imagine?"

Melody shuddered at the thought.

"We had been hearing about all the cool things happening for RADs in Salem, so that's where I went."

Melody almost said she was happy he did.

Thirty minutes later they were standing in front of a black, windowless building, eating meatball subs and drinking super-size sodas.

"What is this place?" she asked.

"Dante's."

"You mean where Stormy Knight played?"

Granite grinned and nodded. "I didn't exactly go straight to Salem after Venue closed. I kind of hung here for a few weeks." He winked, letting her know it was their secret. "That's how I met the Goddesses. We got to talking after their show, and they offered me a job as their roadie, so I split."

Melody tossed her half-eaten food in the trash. "I love how free your life is."

"Have wings, will travel." He winked again.

Wings?

"Come on, I'll show you the inside." Granite took her hand again. This time he didn't let go.

A guy in a black tee and Dickies was pulling chairs off the wood tables. He glanced up when they walked in. "Closed, man."

The place smelled like Pine-Sol and chicken wings.

"Ray. It's me, bro."

"Granite?" He shook his head and came over for a *too-cool-to-hug* one-armed back smack. "Sick of Salem already?"

Granite chuckled. "Just visiting."

While he introduced her to Ray, Melody barely managed to

149

look away from the L7 and Butthole Surfers posters. They would look so cool in her room.

"Mind if I give her a quick tour?"

"Go for it."

Granite held aside a black curtain, heavy with dust. It swung closed behind them, cutting off any last bit of daylight. They headed down a narrow hallway behind the stage that twisted and turned, exactly like Melody's stomach. *Friends hold hands all the time, right?* Melody pulled away and scratched her arm.

"Behold, the greenroom," Granite said. But there was nothing green about it. The smell of stale cigarettes greeted them at the door. "This is where Jeffie Nylons set fire to a refrigerator. Don't ask me how."

A worn burgundy sofa was framed by scorch marks on the white walls. She ran her hand along the charcoal-colored scars. "I saw the footage on YouTube. Were you here?"

"Yup. Never seen anything like it." Granite plopped down on the couch and rested his boots on the smudged glass top of the coffee table. Melody wondered whose famous fingerprints he was stepping on.

A man in a striped button-down and dark, ironed jeans stood in the dark doorway. His brown leather boots and gold accessories earned him the title of Most Hollywood-Looking Dude Ever. "Do I know you?"

Granite jumped to stand. "Mr. Snyder?"

The guy stuck out his hand with mild trepidation. Granite grasped it and shook it like a can of spray paint. "I'm Granite. We met at the Heavens to Betsy gig last month." Mr. Snyder grinned, his overbleached smile a dental homage to the Apple Store. "How could I forget? You're the crack who expects me to believe you've been at every Venue show since the late sixties, right?"

Granite nodded with the pride of being remembered. And then to Melody, "Mr. Snyder is the biggest tour manager in the entire Northwest."

Something began to knock. It was massive opportunity.

"Hey." Melody smiled, shaking his cologne-soaked hand. "My band is actually looking for some summer gigs. I can get you a demo or show you some videos posted on—"

He looked her up and down appraisingly. "Feathers are done, kid." And then to Granite: "You got some chutzpah." He chuckled to himself. "Every show since the sixties, huh?"

Granite nodded.

"So that makes you...what...about seventy years old?"

"Something like that," Granite said, clutching his cool like a winning lottery ticket. Still, this guy was seriously ruffling Melody's feathers. Ha.

"Melody's band is incredibly well known," he offered. "You must have heard of Grunge Go—"

"Leadfeather," she interrupted.

Snyder checked the screen of his BlackBerry and turned to leave. "I told you, kid, feathers are done."

"Wait," Melody called.

Mr. Snyder stopped.

"Look at me...uh..."

"Lew. My first name is Lew."

"Okay, Lew, look at me."

Granite covered his mouth in disbelief. "Melody! What are you—?"

Melody raised her palm to silence him. Some people spend a lifetime searching for a way in. But she had the golden key. Only a fool would refuse to use it.

"You love Leadfeather," she said to Snyder. "You love the name, you love the sound, and you love Granite, their manager."

Lew ran a hand through his thick gray hair. "You bet I do."

Melody took a deep breath. She looked directly into the man's blinking blue eyes and said, "You need to put Leadfeather on tour this summer."

Lew nodded.

"I'm thinking state-of-the-art tour bus, five-star hotels, and pizza money."

Lew poked at the keys on his BlackBerry. He pressed Send. "Wheels are in motion, kid." He pulled a business card out of Granite's ear. "I minor in magic," he boasted. "This one has my personal line. Make sure the rest of the band is free and call me at first light. I want to move on this before the big five book out."

"I couldn't agree more," Granite said. "I'm thinking we should start local, do a couple of smaller shows, then move into Seattle, San Francisco, maybe even LA."

Lew pulled Granite into a headlock and knuckle rubbed his head, "Oy, I love this kid. So full of *shpilkis*." His cell phone chirped. "This is the promoter. We'll talk tomorrow."

Granite played it cool until the door slammed, and then pulled Melody in for a hug. To her, it felt like running into a wall. "That was insane!"

"I know!" she shouted into his neck. "The girls are going to be so excited."

Ping!

She pulled away from Granite and stared at the screen. Her mouth went dry. Her heart began to speed. It's not that she had anything to hide. She and Granite were just friends. Colleagues, really. But how would she explain the summer tour? The snag in the Camp Crescendo plan? The fact that she'd used her Siren powers to alter the plan? She couldn't. So she turned off her phone and put on Granite's helmet. Shutting out the universe once again.

TO: Melody
June 20, 8:43 PM
MOM: WHERE R U?

TO: Mom
June 20, 8:44 PM
MELODY: UPSTAIRS. DOING HOMEWORK! U?

TO: Melody
June 20, 8:44 PM
MOM: DOWNSTAIRS. READING. HOW WAS SCHOOL TODAY?

TO: Mom
June 20, 8:45 PM
MELODY: FINE.

TO: Melody
June 20, 8:45 PM
MOM: FUNNY. I WAS THERE. DIDN'T SEE U.

TO: Mom
June 20, 8:46 PM
MELODY: HUH? WHY WERE U THERE?

TO: Melody
June 20, 8:47 PM
MOM: PRINCIPAL WEEKS CALLED ME IN.

TO: Mom
June 20, 8:47 PM
MELODY: CANDACE AGAIN?

TO: Melody
June 20, 8:48 PM
MOM: U.

TO: Mom
June 20, 8:48 PM
MELODY: ME???

TO: Melody
June 20, 8:48 PM
MOM: U SKIPPED TODAY. FAILED A TEST LAST WEEK, WHICH I GOT HIM TO LET YOU RETAKE, BTW. WHAT'S GOING ON????

TO: Mom
June 20, 8:49 PM
MELODY: I CAN EXPLAIN. I'LL COME DOWN.

TO: Melody
June 20, 8:49 PM
MOM: NO!!!! STAY WHERE YOU ARE. TEXTING ONLY. YOU ARE NOT USING THAT VOICE ON ME AGAIN. NOW TELL ME WHAT'S GOING ON. THE TRUTH.

TO: Mom
June 20, 8:50 PM
MELODY: KINDA JOINED A BAND.

TO: Melody
June 20, 8:50 PM
MOM: WHY DIDN'T YOU TELL ME? MERSTON HAS A GR8 MUSIC PROGRAM.

TO: Mom
June 20, 8:51 PM
MELODY: NOT SCHOOL BAND. A BAND. COLLEGE BAND. SORTA PLAYING AT BARS.

TO: Melody
June 20, 8:52 PM
MOM: HOW R U GETTING INTO BARS?

TO: Mom
June 20, 8:53 PM
MELODY: ONE GUESS.

TO: Melody
June 20, 8:53 PM
MOM: RIGHT. THE VOICE. FORGET I ASKED. BEEN DRINKING? TRUTH!

TO: Mom
June 20, 8:54 PM
MELODY: JUST SINGING. I SWEAR.

TO: Melody
June 20, 8:54 PM
MOM: U HAVE SCHOOL.

TO: Mom
June 20, 8:55 PM
MELODY: IT'S LIFE EXPERIENCE THAT COUNTS.

TO: Melody
June 20, 8:55 PM
MOM: WHAT??? YOU'VE NEVER BEEN LIKE THIS BEFORE.

TO: Mom
June 20, 8:55 PM
MELODY: LIKE WHAT? HAPPY?

TO: Melody
June 20, 8:56 PM
MOM: RUDE. DISHONEST. IRRESPONSIBLE. I'VE NEVER SEEN U LIKE THIS.

TO: Mom
June 20, 8:56 PM
MELODY: EXACTLY. I'VE NEVER GOTTEN IN TROUBLE AT SCHOOL BEFORE. NOT ONCE. SO CAN U CUT ME A BIT OF SLACK?

TO: Melody
June 20, 8:57 PM
MOM: WHY WEREN'T U HONEST WITH ME?

TO: Mom
June 20, 8:57 PM
MELODY: U WOULD'VE SAID NO.

TO: Melody
June 20, 8:58 PM
MOM: I WOULD HAVE ASKED IF YOUR HOMEWORK WAS DONE.

TO: Mom
June 20, 8:58 PM
MELODY: AND IF I SAID YES?

TO: Melody
June 20, 8:59 PM
MOM: I WOULD HAVE ASKED WHAT TIME WE SHOULD BE THERE.

TO: Mom
June 20, 9:00 PM
MELODY: TOMORROW. 9 PM.

TO: Melody
June 20, 9:02 PM
MOM: GET AN A ON THE MAKEUP TEST AND I'LL SEE YOU THERE. ANYTHING LESS AND I'LL MAKE SURE EVERY BAR IN THE PACIFIC NORTHWEST GETS A CRISP COPY OF YOUR BIRTH CERTIFICATE. DEAL?

TO: Mom
June 20, 9:02 PM
MELODY: DEAL.

TO: Melody
June 20, 9:04 PM
MOM: NO MORE LYING! NO MORE SKIPPING SCHOOL. GO STUDY. I'M PUTTING IN EARPLUGS, SO DON'T GET ANY CRAZY IDEAS.

TO: Mom
June 20, 9:04 PM
MELODY: THANK YOU.

CHAPTER SEVENTEEN
RIP, COUNT SLACKULA

The gentle squeak of the hamster's wheel was the only sound in Lala's bedroom. Count Fabulous would be out hunting until dawn, and the other animals had been asleep for hours. Normally, Lala would be snoozing right along with them. But tonight she had skipped her nightly dose of melatonin. Something, her eye-watering yawns reminded her, that would not happen again for at least another millennium.

Exhaustion ached like the flu. The temptation to power down and wing it the next morning was presenting itself with every keystroke. But failing would be much more agonizing than the combined throb of 206 bones. She had to plan every last detail of the T'eau Dally presentation perfectly so that it would all go off without a hitch. The two fashion designers would be judging her school, and she had to make sure the entire experience was a fashion do.

Ping!

Lala glimpsed the iPhone in the shadowy corner of her black lacquer desk.

TO: Lala
June 20, 11:42 PM
CLEO: DID YOU TRY TEXTING? I WAS IN THE SHOWER. SORRY IF I MISSED U. I'M UP THO.

Nice try, Cleo. Lala switched her phone to vibrate. It obviously didn't matter how many times she explained that Weeks wasn't going to call her in the middle of the night with the results of the vote. The royal wouldn't let up.

Ever since Frankie unintentionally outfriended her, Cleo had been intent on winning back her status. Lala tried to figure out which couple the sponsors would respond to more. It was nearly impossible to decide between the two. Both were charming and great-looking. Both were likable and popular. Both represented two worlds coming together in their own ways. But if Cleo won, she'd stop being so competitive with Frankie. So Lala had secretly voted for her and Deuce.

Lala groaned and rested her head in her hands. What did Vlad always say when she felt overwhelmed? *Bite by bite…*

If only she could focus on what needed to get done instead of freak out about what was going to go wrong.…Focus. Focus. Focus.…

Bzzzzzzz.

TO: Lala
June 20, 11:47 PM
CLEO: YOU UP?

Aaarrgghhhhh! Lala tossed her phone onto the bed. Teeny Turner lifted her head and blinked. Lala thought, *I'm sorry,* but was too tired to speak. Instead, she threw her uneaten sesame bar into the trash and turned back to her laptop. *Bite by bite…*

"Tofu?"

"Aaaah!" Lala jumped. "You scared me!"

Vlad stood beside her holding a silver tray. "I knocked, but—"

"It's okay." She smiled softly.

"Thought you might be hungry." He held the tray in front of her face. The earthy smell of his tofu lettuce-wraps brought turbulence to her empty stomach.

"I'm full," she lied.

"Honey, you're Nicole Kidman–pale," he said. "At least take these."

Lala swallowed her iron pills and washed them down with the dregs of her tepid soy latte.

Vlad settled on the edge of Lala's bed, idly petting Teeny on the head. "So I'm working on the proposal for my cookbook—you know, the one where I use only red ingredients—and I'm finally on a roll when…"

Lala poked her fang into her bottom lip. Her uncle was doing the whole *I'm-going-to-hang-around-and-chitchat-until-you-tell-me-what's-on-your-mind* thing. But now the only thing on her mind was the fact that Vlad was in her room chitchatting when she had work to do.

"…your father cruises by and tosses his black coat over the west-facing couch. It was like he was trying to suck my creativity." Vlad pulled off his tortoiseshell glasses and rubbed his gray temples. "Then he drops his briefcase on the loveseat—like work and love are even the slightest bit compatible—and as he's rush-

162

ing around, he stubs his toe on the cactus, nudging the prickly thing right into my harmony path...."

Lala tapped her pen on the notebook. She wanted to be supportive and all, but...

"I'm okay, you know," she finally said. "Just busy with the contest."

"That's a relief." Vlad stood and kissed the top of her head. "Then I guess I'll make like the ends of your hair and split."

"Is that a hint?" Lala asked with a giggle.

"It's time," he said, scissoring his fingers. "Just saying."

"As soon as this is over," Lala said, desperate for a day of beauty and—

The animals began to stir. Hackles went up; tails stiffened; squeaks, slithers, taps, and tweets formed a cyclone of nervous energy that spun around the room.

"What's going on in here?" Mr. D asked from the dim hallway, his trim figure shadowlike and menacing.

"It's okay," Lala said, trying to soothe the mosh pit of creatures. Trying to soothe herself.

"Don't believe her," Vlad whispered, and then slipped past his brother to leave father and daughter alone.

Dressed in a red satin robe and navy cashmere slippers, Mr. D could have passed for a normal dad coming to wish his daughter sweet dreams. If only...

He stepped into the room tentatively. The animals played dead while he surveyed the jumble of crates and bags of birdseed as if seeing them for the first time. *Maybe he is.* Lala couldn't remember a single time he'd come up to her room.

"Nice to see you're back on meat," he finally said, as if she were planning to eat them. "Maybe we'll get some color back in those cheeks." Another round of turbulence rocked Lala's core. "What are you still doing up?" He looked genuinely confused. He was right too. This vamp was big on beauty sleep.

"I'm finalizing my rehearsal schedule for the T'eau Dally visit."

He knit his brows in confusion. *Did he forget?* He tapped a cold hand on her head, duck-duck-goose–style. "Oh yeah, that. When is this rehearsal?"

"Tomorrow," Lala said proudly. "The sponsors come on Thursday."

"Might as well give it your all, I suppose."

Lala turned back to her screen and gripped the mouse to keep from shaking. The words she'd spent hours perfecting began to blur.

"Good luck," he said in a singsongy way that made it impossible to know whether he was serious or skeptical. By the time Lala found the courage to look her father in the eye and maybe even ask if he'd meant it, he was gone.

CHAPTER EIGHTEEN
FAN MALE

Billy was grateful for Spectra's intoxicating lilac-scented sweat, Candace's signature Black Orchid perfume, and Jackson's whirring hand fan. Without which, the smell of teen spirit inside the Underground—a sour blend of chives and oily scalp—could have awoken Kurt Cobain.

The place was packed and pulsating. Fans were jumping like a box of grasshoppers. Leadfeather was playing "Come As You Are" to a sold-out crowd, and the band's passion was infectious.

A satiny-soft peck grazed his cheek. Billy found Spectra and kissed her back.

"Owww!" A stone-faced lug with motorcycle boots had stomped on Billy's foot. "Watch where you're going," he snapped, reaching for his toe.

The stranger looked around for the owner of the foot (and the voice) but quickly gave up and continued pushing toward the stage.

"That guy is so getting laced!" Spectra shouted over Melody's amplified voice.

"It wasn't his fault. He couldn't see Billy," Candace insisted. It was so like her to take the side of the hot stranger.

"I say lace him anyway," Jackson said.

They all glared at him in shock. When had he become a fighter, not a lover?

"What?" Jackson asked shyly. "I don't trust that guy, okay?"

"Looks like Jack is a little jellie," Candace teased.

"What are you talking about?" he snapped, eyes fixed on his feather-clad girlfriend.

"That's Granite, Leadfeather's roadie, and Melody's new—" She stopped herself.

"New what?" Jackson asked, vigorously fanning.

Before Candace could answer, her college boyfriend reached for her arm and pulled her away.

"Don't listen to her. She's just being Candace," Billy said. He knew how gut-wrenching it had felt when he lost Frankie to Brett. He also knew how possible it was to recover. Not that Jackson was going to lose Melody; they were indestructible. Even if she kept watching Granite while she sang. But that was only because she couldn't see Jackson all the way in the back, right?

"Let's move closer to the stage," Billy suggested with a forceful tug.

Jackson fought him off, but invisibles were almost impossible to thwart without looking like a fly-swatting spaz. So he eventually gave in and— "Oof!" Jackson was knocked to the ground by Granite.

"What are you doing?" Billy shouted at the flailing roadie lying on top of his friend.

"I laced him," Spectra tittered in her fairylike voice.

"But how?" Billy asked, remembering a glimpse of the biker's laceless boots.

"Broken guitar string," she said proudly.

Billy accidentally high-fived her shoulder. She accidentally high-fived his jaw in return. They laughed.

Struggling to free Jackson, they untwisted the wire from Granite's boot and pulled him up to standing.

"My fan!" called Jackson, searching the sticky floor. "I can't find my—"

Crunch.

Granite kicked shards of blue-and-white plastic out from under his heel. "Sorry, man," he said, meaning it.

"What did you do?" Jackson yelled, rolling up the sleeves on his plaid button-down.

Billy dashed to his side, just in case a fight broke out. Not that Jackson wasn't strong. He just wasn't as strong as Granite.

"I heard you crying loud, all the way across town…" Melody's clear voice soared over the crowd.

Granite turned toward the stage. "I love Green Day."

"Same," Jackson shouted. "Let's dance!"

That's better.

CHAPTER NINETEEN
THE BUS STOPS HERE

Familiar faces flashed Melody a thumbs-up as she squeezed through the meandering crowd. Each one triggered a flashback from the show she'd just performed: the girl who knew the words to "No Rain"... the guy who shouted, "I love you," after she sang "Creep"... three girls in the front row with feathers... but where was Jackson? She had seen him dancing during the second half of the show and couldn't wait to thank him for his sudden show of support. He said he believed that her trip to Portland with Granite was platonic. He said he had no problem with girls and guys being friends. He said he wasn't mad that she'd missed the T'eau Dally vote. But he hadn't really acted that way until now.

"Melly Belly! Over here!" Glory was waving like a paparazzo. As if her Jimi Hendrix belly shirt, turquoise skinnys, braided leather forehead band, and mother-daughter feather extensions weren't mortifying enough, Beau, in his Clark Kent business suit, was also flagging her over.

"Told you she was our daughter," Glory said to the bartender. He raised his brows, trying to look impressed.

"Ugh, so embarrassing!" Melody giggled. "When will parents realize no one else cares about their kids' accomplishments?"

"When will kids realize parents live to embarrass them?" her father fired back.

Melody had wanted to hide her head in Nine's bass drum when Beau dipped Glory at the end of "Ironic," but humiliation was a small price to pay for their blessing. And it was clear from their sweaty hugs that she had it.

"Let's celebrate!" Glory said. "Baskins?"

Melody scanned the congested area for Jackson. Where was he?

"Negatory," Beau said, wagging a finger. "Dairy is not good for the old pipes. Number one cause of phlegm. I heard Barbra Streisand hasn't had so much as a taste in forty years."

Glory pulled out her iPad, ready to verify. "Lemme check. I think that was Celine."

"That's okay," Melody said. "We have a band meeting now, anyway. I'll be home in an hour."

"How exciting," Glory said, a peacock feather stuck in her lip gloss. "A set list review?"

"No, Granite has a surprise for us. Actually, I'm supposed to meet him now, so…"

After another sweaty hug, Melody began moving through the crowd toward the side door. Along the way, she sent Jackson a text letting him know she'd be in the alley and telling him to join her as soon as he could.

After a single pump of the handle, Melody was enveloped by the humid steam cloud blasting from an air vent. It felt like the

169

bathroom after a Candace shower, only instead of vanilla, it smelled of Merston on lasagna day.

"Hey!" Melody bellowed at the sight of Jackson. He was seated on a rusty paint can beside Cici, Nine, and Granite. "I was looking for you."

"I'm hardly surprised," Jackson said with a confident smirk. His plaid button-down was open halfway to the waist, and his dark hair flopped over his forehead. He looked more relaxed.

"Welcome to the spa," Cici groaned. "May we offer you a complimentary barf bag?" She kicked a mud-soaked KFC bag toward the Dumpster.

Nine-Point-Five laughed.

"Sorry we're slumming," Granite said, tossing Melody a pink Gatorade. "I thought we'd need a little privacy."

Were Jackson and Granite really hanging out? "So you guys know each other?"

"We've been bros ever since the second set," Jackson said, throwing his arm around Granite's brawny shoulder. "This guy knows more about music than I do."

"Not true. He's the one who told me that Soundgarden was named after that statue in Seattle," Granite said.

"But you actually saw—"

"Okay, you two need to stop," Cici joked, her tiara tilting like the Leaning Tower of Pisa.

Nine slapped her a high four-point-five. "Wait, is that the big news?" she asked Granite. "Are you two getting married?"

"We can hold the ceremony at the Hard Rock," Cici teased.

Melody laughed, but for an entirely different reason. Jackson had a boy crush on the guy he'd accused her of liking. *Hey, Alanis, isn't* that *ironic?*

Jackson reached out his hand and pulled her down toward him. "I'm a sucker for a hot lead singer," he said before kissing her with the force of someone who had just returned from war.

Granite turned away.

Jackson didn't smell like the usual waxy pastel crayons. More musty. And a little bit sharp. But he obviously wasn't holding any grudges. So she embraced his new scent; she probably didn't smell so great either.

"OmigodOmigodOmigodOmigod!" Sage burst through the door waving her cell phone. In true Marilyn form, her silver bubble dress rose up from the steam, but unlike the pinup, her legs were covered in red-and-black-striped tights. "I. Just. Got. A. Voice. Mail. From. LEW SNYDER! Hewantstorepusonasummer tourwherewecanfollowallthefestivals!"

Granite smacked his thighs. "And there goes the surprise."

Jackson stood. "The concert promoter?"

Sage bobbled her head.

Cici jumped, the swaying fringes on her knee-high moccasins reminding Melody of a hula skirt. "Shut *up!*"

Nine-Point-Five pressed her drumsticks up against her strawberry-soda pink lips. "Us? As in Leadfeather?"

Sage nodded again.

They grabbed hands and started pogo-ing like twelve-year-olds at a Miley Cyrus concert. Jackson joined in.

Melody looked into Granite's gray eyes. *Really?*

He nodded. *Yes.*

The corners of his mouth twitched toward a smile, but he

171

restrained himself. The conversation with Lew was their secret. Just like that moment of hand-holding.

"Ha!" Melody said, marveling at the power in her voice.

Sage readjusted the blue hair band in her freshly dyed white hair. "He said he already cleared it with our manager and—"

"Manager?" Nine asked.

Granite waved shyly. "Surprise again."

The girls rushed Granite, pulling him onto their pogo. Melody wanted to join them but took Jackson's hand instead. If he hadn't already realized this would crush their summer plans, he was about to. *Why did I tell Lew Snyder to book a summer tour? We could have done some local gigs instead. Or something, anything, that wouldn't break Jackson's heart?*

Sage grabbed her hand. "Aren't you excited?"

Melody nodded toward Jackson, letting her know that this was more complicated than it seemed. But Jackson didn't act heartbroken at all. Instead, he was watching the celebration with an amused look on his face. He probably assumed she was going to say no. Because that's what any responsible, caring, considerate girlfriend would do. *Right?*

"What does he have to do with this?" Sage asked.

So much for nuance.

"It's just that we have these summer plans and—"

"What plans?" Jackson asked, his eyes darker than usual. And then to Granite he added, "Girls just love having commitments."

Granite nodded as if to say he knew exactly what Jackson was talking about.

At least someone did. The Jackson that Melody knew was pumped for Camp Crescendo. Like, *planning-hikes-and-buying-*

matching-Patagonia-fleeces pumped. Maybe he was trying to act cool in front of the band?

"Forget plans. What could possibly be better than a summer tour?" Jackson asked, with his hands up in the air.

Melody's insides swirled. "Really?"

"When Lew Snyder calls, you answer," Jackson said.

"Woooo-hooooo!" cheered her bandmates.

"Now let's go celebrate!" He hooked his arm around Melody's neck and kissed her cheek. "Man, you're smokin' hot."

She giggled.

"Union Tap is playing at the Pigeon Hole," he announced. "You guys want to go?"

The others agreed Melody and Jackson should have some alone time and sent the pair off with a group hug and a Gatorade toast to the summer of rock and roll.

Beyond the steaming alley, the night air was cool, and the breeze on Melody's forehead felt like a much-needed ice-cream headache. A crescent moon shone, lighting their stroll down Liberty Street.

"Are you sure you're okay with this tour?" she asked, now that they were alone.

Jackson shivered and pulled her closer.

"Hello?" She snapped her fingers in front of his face. "Jackson?" Melody grabbed his cold hand. She wanted to make sure he understood how much this meant to her. How much he meant to her. "Thank you for being so supportive."

"Sure." He smiled politely, as if they had just met. "You really were great tonight."

"Is that why you're okay with this? Because you believe in me?" she asked, stopping outside the Pigeon Hole. She wasn't particularly into seeing live music. She had just *been* the live music and had that heavy feeling that follows a long cry. Besides, she needed to get home. But if Jackson was so eager to support her interests, she would make every effort to support his. He must have studied up on her favorite bands to know that fact about Soundgarden.... *Wait a second....*

He shivered again and buttoned up his shirt. "I told you, Melly, I'm okay with you being in this band."

Melody stiffened. "What about the tour?"

"What tour?"

Melody's heart began to sprint. Her mouth dried. She grabbed Jackson's hands in hers. "Where are we going right now?"

He looked at the fogged window of the bar. Glanced up at the swinging wood sign. "The Pigeon Hole?" he read.

Melody's heart dropped toward her pink Chucks. "Where's your fan?"

Jackson shrugged. "That oaf Granite stepped on it. I knew that guy had it in for me."

He shut his hazel eyes, as if closing them might make it all go away. If only...

He sighed. "D.J. was here, wasn't he?"

Melody nodded. Her eyes stung with disappointment. How could she have missed the signs?

"What happened?"

174

Melody sighed. "Leadfeather got booked on a summer tour. You were happy for me. You told me to do it."

He dropped her hand and shook his head. "You mean D.J. did."

"How was I supposed to know?" Melody snapped back.

Jackson rolled his eyes. "How long have you known me, Melody? Didn't you suspect that maybe, possibly, asking me loaded questions in a superhot bar was a little, oh, I don't know, problematic?"

Fury hardened the tears behind Melody's eyes. "In case you hadn't noticed, I was a little busy in there."

Jackson dug his car keys out of his pocket and made a fist around them. "Actually, I had noticed. You've been too busy for anything that doesn't have to do with this band."

Ugh! "This band," she practically spat, "happens to be a dream come true for me."

"Well, I would never want to come between you and your dreams," he shouted. And then, "Good luck on your tour." He turned to leave.

"What about us?" she called.

He stopped. His expression had melted to sadness. "What about us?"

"Is that it?"

"Do you want it to be?"

A couple, arm in arm, teetered by, giggle-talking the way only people in love can do. Melody wanted to trip them. "No."

"Then prove it," he said, and walked away.

CHAPTER TWENTY
SHOCK AND *KA*!

Bwoop. Bwoop.

The homeroom bell rang. Not that Frankie needed a reminder to get to class. She'd been sitting in that wooden seat for eleven minutes, staring at motivational posters of vistas and rainbows until they blurred. Waiting. Sparking.

Principal Weeks was about to announce the winner of the T'eau Dally vote. And Frankie didn't want to miss it. Not because she had any chance of winning. Cleo's purchase of Haylee and Heath's campaign speech had guaranteed that. But because she didn't want to look like a sore loser. Feeling like one was painful enough.

"Good luck," said Clawdeen and Blue when they came in. Others communicated their well wishes with closemouthed smiles, prolonged glances, or encouraging pats on the back. But there was a mournful quality behind their gestures. A *sorry-for-your-loss* kind of thing.

"Stop tugging!" Brett said, sitting at the desk beside her. "We haven't lost yet."

Yet.

An orange tee and khaki shorts slipped into the seat behind her. "You excited, Stein?" Billy asked.

"Totally," Frankie managed, despite the orb of depression in the back of her throat. She eked out a weak smile to prove her enthusiasm.

She would congratulate Cleo and Deuce on their win and carry on as if being named the T'eau Dally It Couple wasn't the ultimate way to kick off the summer. Like free footwear for life was nothing to get charged up about. As though professional photographs of her and Brett wouldn't be cherished by their kids. She would follow her parents' advice and accept defeat like a winner....Defeat...de-feat...da feet...the feet...the feet that won't wear T'eau Dally shoes... "Stop!"

"Stop what?" Brett asked, gripping her forearm. Grounding her.

"Um..." Frankie said to his hand. "I meant, stop, where did you get that voltage blue nail polish?"

He released his hold. "You bought it for me."

Oops. "And don't you forget it."

"Don't you," he teased.

"Don't you," she teased back.

"Don't you."

"Don't—"

The classroom door opened with a bang. Cleo stood in the doorway, one hand on her hip, the other swaying languidly at her side. Any more chill and it would have fallen from her purple-and-gold maxidress like an icicle and shattered on the linoleum. Even Cleo's outfit was relaxed.

A few girls began applauding when they saw her, Blue and Clawdeen among them, part of their ongoing efforts to remain T'eau Dally supportive to both sides. Cleo quickly raised her palm. "Not yet." At least she wasn't 100 percent sure she'd won. And then, "Wait for Deucey." Cleo finger-combed her thick black bangs, pursed her glossed lips, and posed for a camera that wasn't there.

Billy leaned forward and mumbled, "She should be on TV."

"Why?" Frankie asked, aware of the jealousy in her voice.

"So I could turn her off."

Brett snickered. Frankie wanted to but refused. Giggling would only make her seem threatened. Instead, she stared at the ink stains on her desk and tried not to look any more green than usual.

"Now you can clap," Cleo announced when Deuce appeared by her side. She hooked her arm through his and led him toward the back of the class, as if oblivious to the fanfare. Her walk down the aisle—assured and steady—seemed more rehearsed than Kate Middleton's. And Deuce's outfit—a black cashmere beanie, gold Carreras, and crisp gray Diesels—was more studied than Prince William's.

Frankie picked the lavender polish off her thumbnail. Because, really, who cared?

Mrs. Simon strode in, her thighs swishing like windshield wipers. She clapped briskly. "Seats."

Cleo and Deuce picked up their pace, but only a little.

Frankie rested her head on her desk. Billy rubbed her back.

The white speaker above the chalkboard crackled to life. Cleo clutched the lucky bronze scarab hanging around her neck.

"Goooooooood mooooooorning, Merston High!" boomed Principal Weeks.

Losing was one thing, but did it have to be amplified? Couldn't he send an e-mail?

"Happy Wednesday," Weeks bellowed. "Remember, we only have three more days of school..."

Someone moaned. Ghoulia?

"...so let's make them count. Speaking of count, that's all I've been doing. I counted and counted and counted your votes."

Frankie lifted her head. Smile. Project confidence. Gritting her teeth, she raised her chin and braced herself for the inevitable punch. Brett flashed her a supportive grin. *We tried.*

Weeks cleared his throat into the PA. "Now, without further delay..."

"Get ready. This is it," Billy said with a pat on her back. "And the Oscar goes to..."

"Stop," Frankie hissed.

"Actually"—Weeks paused—"I'm going to have Lala make the announcement."

Everyone moaned.

"Hey." Lala giggled nervously. "The couple you chose to represent Merston High is..."

Cleo's chair scraped along the floor. *Is she already standing?*

"Brett Redding and Frankie Stein!"

What?

Frankie stared at Brett. He stared back. His eyes were wide. Her bolts were firing. Her ears began to ring. Were people clapping or booing? Was Cleo demanding a recount? Were Blue and Clawdeen still T'eau Dally supportive of both sides? Or had they finally allowed their true feelings to show? Frankie was too shocked to tell.

The only thing she remembered before passing out was Billy tickling her ear with a warm whisper as he said, "Told you that you'd win, Stein. Told you."

CHAPTER TWENTY-ONE
STRESSED TO KILL

Thump.

A basketball landed an inch away from Jackson's can of red paint. That's all they needed—a gym floor that looked like a crime scene.

"Can't you play somewhere else?" Lala shouted at Davis Dreyson.

"You mean somewhere other than the gym?" he asked, scooping up the ball with his orangutanish arm. The sneaker-squeaking quickly resumed. Lala's headache intensified. KEEP BOUNCING BALLS AWAY FROM PAINT CANS was not on her to-do list. Neither was FORCE TEAM TO WORK FASTER, yet there she was, staring at a mostly blank canvas.

It was supposed to boast the new T'eau Dally logo. Instead, it looked more like a baboon butt in the middle of a giant diaper.

Lala lifted the brim of her BeDazzled SUPERVISOR visor (a punny gift from Clawdeen) and forced a patient smile. "Jackson, what's taking so long? They'll be here tomorrow. So far you just have the—" Lala tilted her head. "What is that, anyway? And what about drying time? Have you factored that in?"

Jackson dabbed his brush in the paint can, scraped the excess off on the side, and mumbled, "It'll be ready. Don't worry."

Typical artist.

Still, Lala tapped her iPad screen and added a check mark to the box beside NEW LOGO. So what if it wasn't T'eau-Dally done? Jackson said it would be. And she needed to feel that they were making progress.

Bite by bite…

CATWALK was next.

Clawd was in the far corner of the gym (*thanks, selfish basketball players!*) lifting a sheet of plywood toward the frame. Either his arms were trembling or he happened to be standing on an active fault line. He was swaying back and forth as though he was about to drop the board. Lala ran over to help.

She had once read about a mother whose baby was trapped under a car. Apparently, the power of love had filled the woman with enough strength to lift the car and rescue her child. Well, this contest was like her baby, so wouldn't it make sense that she could just grab a corner of the plywood and lift?

"What are you doing?" Clawd grunted. He began to teeter.

"I'm saving you," she grunted back. And then, "Owie!" A splinter lodged its way into the tip of her iPad finger. So much for checking boxes on her to-do list.

Lala let go and began fang-poking the affected area. (*Where's a pin when you need one?*)

The sudden movement threw Clawd off balance, and the board came smashing down.

182

"Awoooo!" Clawd howled through clenched teeth. "What were you thinking?" he growled, rubbing his shoulder.

"Is it broken?" Lala asked.

Clawd rotated his arm in tiny circles. "Fractured, maybe. Or bruised. I should probably go see the—"

"Not you, the board!" Lala snapped. "Look, there's a crack right down the middle. Can we replace it by tomorrow? Because that's a liability. That thing could split when the models are walking on it."

"Great point," Clawd said. "Forget my football arm. I'm rabid concerned about the board. That board was, like, everything to me."

Awww. Lala lifted up on tippy-toes and kissed him on the cheek. Right there in the middle of everyone. Even though he hated that kind of thing, she wanted him to know how much she appreciated his putting her contest before his own body. "Don't worry too much. Go ice. I'll find someone else to replace it. I'll let you know when the new one gets here."

Beep. Lala's pink G-Shock rang. Twenty-four-point-two-five hours to go.

As long as nothing went wrong, by the time the T'eau Dally people walked through those double doors, she'd be as ready to impress as a bachelorette in the season finale. Two red items blinked from her iPad scheduler.

REVIEW CLAWDEEN'S T'EAU DALLY HIGH DIY ACTIVE WEAR.

ACCEPT DELIVERY OF SHOES.

Thank you, personal-assistant-slash-iPad. Where is Clawdeen? And where are those shoes?

Dickie Dally had promised two pairs for the It Couple. Which is why Frankie and Brett were sitting on the bleachers, waiting to practice their walk. Which would now have to be done in socks and on the floor, thanks to that shoddy board.

Bite by bite…

Under the bleachers, Clawdeen and her sewing klatch were gathered like trolls. *At least someone is on track.* Maybe the sight of perfection would settle the bagel-storm brewing in her stomach. "Hey, Deenie," Lala said, poking her head in. Her friend's curls were frizzed like a "before" photo, and she was wearing her plaid sleepover pajamas. "You okay?"

"Take five," Clawdeen told her crew. "Blue, stay with me."

"Roger, Sheila," she said, spritzing her scales with a squirt gun.

The girls filed out quickly. Rubbing their backs and squinting, they emerged into the light.

"Five means five," Lala called after them. "Not a minute more." And then, "So, how's it going?"

Blue reached across the heap of material, thread tangles, and felt scraps. She rested a hand on Lala's cashmere-covered arm. "La, ya have to promise ya won't go all bonkers."

Bonkers? Why would I go bonkers? You mean because your DIY looks like DI-crap?

"I promise," Lala lied through her fangs.

Clawdeen reached behind her back. "So, I've never done iron-ons, right?"

Lala's splinter began to throb, and it felt like someone was jabbing a stake behind her right eye. She fumbled for her iron pills and popped two.

"Well…" Clawdeen glanced at Blue. "My iron runs a little hot, so…" She held up a pair of gray athletic shorts. Across the

184

butt were wrinkled black letters that spelled … Lala looked more closely.

T' AU L
E DA

What did that spell?

The edges of the *T* and the *E* curled up and exposed the white lining underneath. Lala closed her eyes. She counted backward from thirteen and took a deep breath. Even though she felt like ripping the letters off with her fangs, she managed to control herself. "Okay. It's going to be okay. We still have time."

Clawdeen sighed. "Don't worry, these will look perfect by tomorrow. Where there's a Wolf, there's a way, right?"

I hope so.

Lala glanced at her watch. Seven minutes left in first period. Seven minutes until Frankie and Blue were due in gym class and Brett had chem lab.

Where are the shoes?

On the off chance that they had been delivered to the office, Lala hurried down the hall. She passed signs for the TOE DALLY

HIGH CAFETERIA, the TOE DALLY HIGH LIBRARY, and the TOE DALLY HIGH TEACHERS' LOUNGE.

"Seriously?" she shouted.

"Feeling a bit'a preshy, are we?" Blue asked, catching up.

Lala nodded. She wanted to cry. Or scream. Or DIY-die. *And where are those SHOES?*

"If I mess this up, my dad's going to say, 'I told you so,' and send us all to Radcliffe next year." She hugged her iPad to her chest, wishing it were Count Fabulous.

Blue pulled a bottle of coconut oil out of her canvas tote and slathered her arms. "You'll be all right. You still have a whole day to get ready."

Lala kept moving. She needed those shoes. Something needed to go right.

"Did I ever tell you about my birthday walkabout?"

Lala shook her head.

"We were s'posed to have this bonzer barbie at the end, right? Only Pops got lost. So there we were, ten screaming sheilas in the middle of the bush. And everything's goin' wrong. We're crossing this billabong, and the crocs are pulling out left and right. Mum forgets the eskie, so we don't have any grub. Then we spot this reservoir and hop in to cool off. Only it's snapping with bitin' prawns. Even Pops was yellin' like a kookaburra."

Lala stopped and stared. What, exactly, was the point?

"Finally, this fat joey hops by and gets me thinking. Judging from the size of that bugger's belly, he knows where the barbie is. So we followed him. And ended up at the Outback Golf Club, where it was meat pies and iced sammies for everyone."

They passed a TOE DALLY HIGH BAND sign. If her entire future didn't depend on winning this contest, Lala might have laughed.

"All I'm saying," continued Blue, "is sometimes life shoots you a gutser. But if you keep your eyes on the joey, she'll be all meat pies and sammies in the end."

Lala giggled. "What happened to the joey?"

Blue smiled. "Ah, this part is ace! The next morning he showed up on our porch. Mum gave him Jazzy's room when he went off to college. Been there for nine years."

Nothing calmed Lala like an animal story with a happy ending. (At least she thought it was an animal story.) And so she entered the office with a smile.

"Anyone here named Lala?" asked a hefty guy in a brown button-down and wrinkle-resistant shorts. A box big enough for two pairs of shoes rested on his abdomen.

"That's me!" She felt like hugging the man but decided a heart drawn next to her signature would suffice.

She ripped off the tape, grabbed hold of a fake leather strap, and yanked it free. Styrofoam chunks flurried to the floor.

"Call me a dill, but what are those?" Blue asked.

"Packing peanuts," Lala explained. "They're used in America to keep stuff in boxes from bumping around." She lowered her voice. "Terrible for the environment."

Blue's blue eyes were wide, and her blond brows arched in confusion. "No, those!" She pointed at the boot in Lala's hand.

Lala giggled. The highly anticipated hybrid was unlike anything they'd ever seen before. The foot slid into an ankle-high tube-shaped area. In front of which was a wide pouch. A chocolate-brown strap that held a matching change purse wrapped around the center like a ribbon cinched around a paper bag. Grayish brown and soft as a teddy bear, it looked more like an open satchel than a shoe. The female version had rubber treads and a two-inch heel that curved at the bottom like a tail. The male's was flat and wide, similar to a skater sneaker.

"I reckon I could keep my hand cream in there," Blue said, examining the pouch.

Lala giggled. Blue was right. Who needed a tote when she had a T'eau Dally? These shoes were bound to revolutionize women's fashion. But men's? More like feminize. She had a hard time imagining Clawd wearing something so...European. Or any athlete, for that matter. Any American male. But Dally was the number one sports-apparel brand for a reason. If Dickie—a chiseled sports wunderkind—put his name on something, it didn't matter what the item looked like. Plaid soccer shorts, knee-high basketball shoes, clear baseball bats—no one asked questions. The unconventional gear outperformed anything they had used in the past, and that's all they needed to know.

By the time Lala found Frankie, she and Brett were racing to their next class.

"Voltage!" Frankie said, hugging the shoes to her chest.

"Try them on," Lala urged. "Make sure they fit."

"I will, after this period. But don't worry. I can walk in anything." She pointed the toe of her striped platform Mary Janes. "See?"

Lala gave the other pair to Brett. He pinched them between his fingers and held them up to the fluorescent lights. "What are these?"

"He's not much of a jock," Frankie said, justifying the confusion. "We'll practice walking in them tonight."

Lala squeeze-thanked Frankie so tight that she almost popped a bolt. Finally, someone she could count on.

Bite by bite...

As the halls cleared, Lala tapped her iPad to life and got started on a new to-do list.

The more she typed, the more Lala realized that Blue was right. Everything could be fixed. There was still time. Meat pies and iced sammies were still in her future....

And then, *slam!* She bashed straight into two grown-ups. Scalding coffee from their venti to-go cups splattered all over their clothing. Lala's iPad crashed to the floor.

"Ahhhh!" the couple screamed. And then they began cursing, he in English and she in...French!

Oh no. Oh no no no no no....

The brown stained VISITOR stickers on their shirts immediately confirmed Lala's fear: Her guests had arrived twenty-one hours and fourteen minutes early.

Time of social death: 9:46 AM.

CHAPTER TWENTY-TWO
SHOE D'ETAT

As it turned out, gym class was the perfect solution to Frankie's PDA problem. A public display of axhilaration—or was it spelled *exhilaration*?—would be like rubbing her victory in Cleo's face. And that was not the Stein way. But suppressing the desire to scream "IwonIwonIwon" was like stifling a finger spark—a force too mighty to control.

Fencing, however, offered the ideal compromise. When Frankie lifted her mask for some fresh air, she tried to appear blasé, as if becoming the T'eau Dally High It Couple just meant more responsibility, less fun. Once behind the mask, she smiled and squealed like the new American Idol. The shock of winning still hadn't worn off. It was almost as if she could feel it snapping and zapping inside her white jacket. Had she and Brett really gotten more votes? Than Cleo and Deuce? In a popularity contest? What next? Outscoring Kourtney Kardashian 96 percent to 4 percent in the "Who Wore It Best?" section of *Us Weekly*?

At least Cleo hadn't been in math class when Mr. Beeder gave

Frankie a tray of doughnuts from the teachers' lounge. And Cleo hadn't been in music class when Ms. Andrews taught "We Are the Champions" in Frankie's honor. In fact, Cleo had skipped most of the morning, claiming she had a meeting at *Teen Vogue*. But she was there now. Taking five from her duel to reapply her gloss. Grinning as if she had a secret too delicious to share. Viveka said that was to be expected. It was called "saving face." From where Frankie was lunging, it looked more like "gas face."

In the locker room, Frankie peeled off her white suit and wrapped herself in a heather gray robe.

"Are those the shoes?" Clawdeen asked, a stuck comb dangling from her hair.

Six towel-wrapped girls crowded around the open locker for a better view. Cleo rolled her eyes and squirted more oil onto her legs.

"They're ace!" Blue called, even though she'd already seen them.

"Have you tried them on?"

"Are they hard to walk in?"

"What are you going to wear with them?"

"They totally suit you."

"I knew they would. That's why I voted for you."

"I voted for you too."

"I didn't, but I'm still glad you won."

Cleo was three lockers down, pretending to read funny texts from very important people. Her endless attempts to "save face" tugged at Frankie's heart space. If the princess felt half as humiliated as Frankie did when she thought she had lost...

"Can we talk about it later?" Frankie asked, closing her locker. "Today's gym class kinda drained me, so..."

All the girls returned to their hair-drying stations.

"How much do you love?" Spectra whispered in Frankie's ear.

"They're pretty mint," Frankie said, peeking at the gray-brown booties.

"Not those," she hissed. And then she tilted her head toward Cleo, who was wrapping her wrists in linen, no one by her side but a heap of wet towels. "That?"

"Huh?" Frankie asked the lilac-scented air.

"We finally gave her what she deserved." Spectra giggled, her chains rattling.

"I have no idea what you're—"

"Don't worry," Spectra whispered. "No one can hear us over those hair dryers. And Billy hasn't told anyone."

"Told anyone what?" Frankie asked, circling her neck bolt with a Q-tip.

Spectra giggled. "That Billy and I switched the ballot boxes so you'd win."

Tzzzz. The Q-tip caught fire. Frankie blew it out and waved away the scent of burned cotton. Still, something smelled off.

"You did what?"

"He didn't tell you?"

Frankie twisted her matted hair into a knot. It now matched the one in her stomach. The vote was fixed? She hadn't actually won? She slammed her locker shut. Served her right to think she'd ever beat Cleo. To think that she'd ever beat anyone. Salty shame drops spilled down her cheeks. *I failed. Again.*

Warm, lilac-scented arms enveloped her like a bubble bath.

"I'm going to go tell Cleo," Frankie said.

Spectra's surprisingly strong hand grabbed her bare arm. "You

192

can't, Frankie! We'll get in so much trouble. Besides, she'll just gloat. Who wants to see that?"

Clawdeen finished grooming her fur to a glossy shine and clicked off the dryer just as Spectra was completing her thought, leaving the ghoul's words dangling like participles. "Who wants to see what?"

"Um, the rash between my toes," blurted Spectra.

Clawdeen winced. "Pass."

Frankie pulled the T'eau Dally shoes out of her locker. She stroked the supple material one last time, kissed them good-bye, and then crossed the aisle. Cleo—now wrapped, oiled, kohled, and glossed—was packing up for third period.

"Here," Frankie said, thrusting the boots toward her. "I'm out."

Cleo narrowed her eyes.

"It's true," Frankie said. "I'm resigning." Spectra's words rang in her head like a smoke alarm.

"Why?" Cleo asked, backing away. "What's wrong with them?" She peered into the pouch with an upturned lip. "Ew, wait. Did Spectra try those on? They're all rashy, aren't they?"

Frankie finger-drew an invisible X across her robe. "Cross my bolts and hope to fry."

Bwoop. Bwoop.

Hair dryers stopped. Lockers slammed shut. But no one left. One by one, they began to stall, lurking in the background, waiting to see who would end up with the coveted shoes.

Bwoop. Bwoop.

Cleo slung her bag over her oiled shoulder. "Well, something must be wrong with them."

"Nothing is wrong with them. I swear. Brett's not that into it.

193

And I've got a lot of family stuff going on." Frankie took a deep breath. "You and Deuce have been here longer than I have. If anyone should represent Merston—"

"*Ka!*" Cleo turned on the toe of her three-inch wooden platform. "I don't want your charity." And then she made like a Stein and bolted.

"Cleo, wait!" Still in her robe, Frankie stuffed her clothes into a bag. Her hair was matted. Her neck smelled like burned cotton. Her makeup had been smudged to black-eye proportions. Still, she took to the crowded halls with the confidence of someone who didn't look like a mug shot.

"It's not charity. You deserve this," Frankie shouted at the glossy black hair escaping into the crowd.

"Frankie, stop it," insisted Spectra, lingering like lilac-scented air freshener. "You deserve this too."

"If I deserved it, I would have won," Frankie snapped. She took off at a sprint. "They're yours. Take them," she called out after Cleo.

Cleo stopped outside her English class. Her topaz eyes bore into Frankie's. No longer alive and glinting, they had become two hard marbles. "I. Don't. Want. Them."

Frankie shoved them into Cleo's tote. "Just take them."

"I told you, I don't want your rashy charity shoes." Cleo whipped them back at her.

"Heads!" someone called as the shoes sailed through the air.

"Ahhhh!"

Students scattered.

The shoes thumped to the linoleum, just like Frankie's ego space. Why would Billy fix the results? Had she really given him the impression that it was better to cheat than lose?

Frankie thought back on her behavior since the contest started. She had altered her style, given away her father's bolts, and drained her energy to charge a bunch of soulless electronics. For what? A career as a spokesmodel? The chance to show Cleo she was worthy of 607 virtual friends? The ability to say she'd finally won?

What was so great about winning, anyway? Frankie was a plays-well-with-others kind of girl. And so far, being number one just meant hiding her true feelings underwater. It meant others felt like losers when she was around. It meant more separation, when all she'd ever wanted was to fit in.

She nudged the shoes toward Cleo, jutted her chin in the air, and marched back to the locker room, confident that this time, losing was a win-win.

CHAPTER TWENTY-THREE
A SIGHT FOR FOUR EYES

Summer was descending on Merston. Windows were propped open, as if daring them to escape. And like a Siren's song, the sun-scented breeze had a call few could resist.

Melody was one of the few who resisted. What was the point? Skipping merrily in the sun was for lovers and giddy best friends, not the recently dumped or the girl whose parents had just been called to the principal's office.

She violently yanked her free weight of a history textbook from her almost empty locker, as if it were responsible for her standoff with Jackson. She'd spent all weekend hoping he'd realize how selfish he'd been and apologize. But a ticking clock had been the only action her iPhone had seen for days. If stubbornness were a race, she and Jackson would be tied for first. The only thing keeping her going was the vanilla latte with whip she'd guzzled at lunch, and dreaming about the upcoming tour. Three more days and then *Melody out*!

"Melly!" called a familiar voice. Candace ran stiffly toward

Melody in her turquoise Prada wedges. Dressed in a striped romper with bright summer beads swaying around her neck, she looked like an escaped mannequin attempting to move for the first time. "You can get a ride home with Jackson, right?" She closed her fist around the car keys, making it clear that this wasn't so much a question as a situation update.

Melody's chest tightened, missing the days when she could have answered yes. "Where are you going?"

Candace paused to let the passing students fall out of eavesdropping range. "Shane and I want to grab a bite before our Greek Mythology lecture."

Seriously? "Candace, how can you have a lecture? You don't even go to that college."

"Have you seen the size of those classes? There are, like, three hundred people in them. The professor has no clue. Shane and I text the whole time. It's the cutest. So, you're good for a ride?"

"Yeah, I'll figure it out."

"Wait," Candace said, twirling coral beads around her finger. "Are you still giving Jackson the silent treatment because he left you outside the Pigeon Hole?"

If only it were that simple. "He's waiting for me to prove my love."

"And you don't love him anymore," Candace concluded like a seasoned therapist. "It happens."

"No," Melody said, finally able to see past her anger. Or was it her ego? "I *do*. It's just that…" What was it, exactly? *I don't want to sacrifice my dreams for his? I don't want him to want me to? I hate missing him?* "I think the only proof he'll accept is me walking away from this tour and—"

197

Candace gasped. "An ultimatum? Did he give you an ultimatum?"

"Not in so many words, but—"

Candace slapped a locker. It echoed through the near-empty hall. "No one gives a Carver girl one of those," she said, like it was an STD. She slid her red Wayfarers on. "Well then, if he wants you to prove your love, go ahead. Prove your love."

"Huh?"

"Yeah, prove your love for that hot roadie, Granite. That guy is a fuh-ox."

Melody giggled.

"When Jackson busts you, say, 'Ohhhh, you meant prove my love for *you*. Ooops, sor-reeee!'"

Jackson was above games, and so was Melody. But it was funny to consider. Or maybe it was just funny that she was in the position to make one guy jealous with another. Not ha-ha funny. More like, *Who would have thought?*

Bwoop. Bwoop.

"I gotta go," Candace said with the urgency of an outlaw. "You'll be okay getting home?"

Melody nodded. "Enjoy the lecture." She turned on the toe of her black Converse, headed toward another of Mr. Chan's lessons on how World War II applies to social media. While checking her texts—maybe Jackson missed her too—Melody slammed into him.

"Hey!" he blurted. And then, as if remembering their situation, he stiffened.

He was with Lala and two coffee-coated strangers. One was a model-tall stick of a woman in a buttery-yellow leather tank and

198

black leather pants. Her patent stilettos were studded with tiny silver spikes. Beside her was a blond marshmallow of a guy in a tight white tracksuit. They were one square of chocolate and a graham cracker away from a s'more.

As Jackson pretended to be fascinated with something in the distance, Lala pulled Melody forward. "Mel, I'd like you to meet Brigitte T'eau and Dickie Dally."

The marshmallow was Dickie Dally? Athlete? Figurehead? Playboy? This MVP was F-A-T. "Hey," Melody managed, and then tried to make a move toward history class.

But Lala's cold hand yanked her back. "Melody is the lead singer of Leadfeather. She'll be a big part of the T'eau Dally Talented music department once she gets back from her tour."

Jackson made a closed-mouth sneezing sound. Melody's stomach clenched.

Brigitte pursed her plum-stained lips. "*Magnifique*," she purred. "*J'aime vos plumes*," she added while fingering the feathers in Melody's hair. Melody stood still and repressed the urge to shrug her off.

"Someone likes to hunt," Dickie said with a phlegmy chortle.

"And that someone just so happens to be Jackson's girlfriend!" Lala smiled brightly.

Melody gasped. "Actually—"

"Ha! That's my boy!" Dickie elbowed Jackson in the ribs. Jackson dropped his phone. Melody dropped her jaw.

"So tell me, Jake," said Marshmallow, "does this early bird get the worm? Ha!"

Ew!

"Foul!" snapped Brigitte.

"Pun intended!" Dickie shouted, delighted. "Get it? Bird? Fowl?"

It was clear from Brigitte's *I-smell-sour-milk* face that she didn't.

"We're on a break," Jackson said.

Melody stared at him. That was like piling on deodorant and calling it a shower. "I'd say it's more like a break*up*."

"Good to know," Jackson said, swiping a finger across his iPhone. "Mind if we take five while I update my status on Facebook?"

"Ha! Does this mean you're single?" Dickie asked Melody.

Brigitte *tsk-tsk*ed and patted Melody's shoulder.

"I guess it does," she said to Jackson.

"Don't act so surprised. It was your idea."

"Which part? Leaving me outside a bar in the middle of the night or making me feel guilty for following my dream?"

"Only you can make you feel guilty," Jackson said smugly.

"And only you would say something that pretentious," Melody fired back.

Lala's dark eyes were wide with horror. "How 'bout we move along and finish the tour, Jackson?"

"Sounds great," he barked, and then took off down the hall. Lala and Brigitte hurried to catch him. Dickie shoulder-checked Melody into the wall. "Call me when you graduate college." He winked and then *swish-swish*ed away in all his nylon glory.

Frothing with anger, Melody couldn't imagine sitting still for a Chan lecture. Instead, she hurried to her locker and opened it just so she could kick it shut again. And then she did it again. And again. And—

Ping.

Melody fumbled to fish her phone from the pocket of her cut-offs. Finally, an apology.

TO: Melody
June 22, 10:17 AM
GRANITE: MEET ME ON THE ROOF.

TO: Granite
June 22, 10:17 AM
MELODY: LOVE TO.

The metal security door had slammed shut behind her. A warm wind whipped her ponytail and sent feathers scattering across the concrete roof. Did Jackson seriously think this was her fault?

"Hey, you," called Granite, leaning against the humming air-conditioning unit.

Melody hurried toward him, grateful for the distraction.

"Look," he said, taking her hand and walking her to the edge. His dark gray pocket tee brought out the green in his stone-colored eyes. Her heart began to speed again. "Everything looks so different up here." He pointed his sinewy forearm toward the Riverfront. The carousel spun in a slow circle like a music box. Behind it, the Willamette River ran smooth as a hot caramel stream.

"It's like a model city," she said as people scurried down Main Street like Guatemalan worry dolls. She tried to imagine what they might be stressing about. Boyfriends? Jobs? Family? The little things seemed less important from this perspective. "I can't believe I've never been up here before."

"Gargoyles always have a penthouse view. But you"—he turned to face her—"you've wasted so much time trapped in this box." He gestured to the building beneath their feet. "Once you go high, you begin to realize that nothing can hold you down."

"Well, there is gravity," she joked.

He rolled his eyes playfully and then took her hand. "You have hundreds of choices. Millions of options. You just have to step outside and look around."

This time Melody allowed herself to look deep into Granite's eyes. Maybe he was right. She *did* feel stuck lately—between school and Leadfeather, Camp Crescendo and the tour, Jackson and Gra—

He hooked his index finger through her belt loop and tugged her closer. She tucked her hair behind her ears. He ran a finger down her cheek and lifted her chin. His eyes reflected the summer sun like pebbles in a clear mountain stream. He leaned closer. Melody did not.

I don't do things like this. Candace does. I don't play games. I don't hook up on rooftops. Ultimatums don't lead to make-outs. Love does. And I don't love Granite. I love Jackson....

But I like Granite. I like him a lot. We both share a passion for music and have lived most of our lives on the fringes, surrounded by the action but rarely a part of it. He is hot. I have wondered what it would be like to kiss him. Jackson has updated his status to single and... And somehow they found each other.

Granite's kiss was strong and assured, passionate and consuming. Honking horns from the traffic below riffed with her thumping heart, creating what she'd come to think of as "their song." She and Jackson were officially done. She was moving on. This kiss was good. Really good. Tingly, curl-your-toes satisfying. But it was different....

Making out with Granite was like tossing back a hot espresso. With Jackson it was more like sipping a white chocolate mocha. By a fireplace. Under a soft blanket and—

Bam!

The metal door slammed again. Melody instinctively pulled back and opened her eyes. Jackson, Lala, Brigitte, and Dickie were standing by the open door.

"Looks like this bird has flown the nest," Dickie announced.

Lala covered her mouth with both hands. Brigitte flashed Melody a French thumbs-up.

Jackson powered up his hand fan and turned away. "Over here is where we'll put the T'eau Dally High observation deck," he said, leading them to the north edge of the building, taking the warmth of the day with him.

Granite brushed the hair off her face and smiled. "Looks like everyone's moved on." He pulled her in for another kiss.

Once again, she wasn't sure if she should let him.

And then she kissed him back.

CHAPTER TWENTY-FOUR
T'EAU-DALLY STONED

Bite by bite, Lala told herself as she led her guests down from the rooftop. Sadly, the only three words that could calm her now would be "Congratulations, you won." But Dickie would fit into Brigitte's faux-leather pants before that ever happened. Frankie, their spokesmodel, wasn't answering her texts, the gym looked like an abandoned construction site, and Jackson and Melody were more drama than daytime TV. Oh, and then there was the whole *bumping-into-the-clients-and-spilling-hot-coffee-all-over-them* incident. And the *none-of-this-would-have-happened-if-you-didn't-show-up-a-day-early* fiasco. The only thing left to do now was hope that her father hadn't moved the Merston yearbook out of her success space. Assuming fang shui even worked.

"No, really," Jackson told Brigitte, his voice vibrating against the whirring blades of his hand fan. "I'm fine. It was time to move on anyway. We were drifting."

Dickie smacked him on the back. "Ha! Spoken like a true player."

Jackson tried to flash a winning smile. It looked like he was holding in barf.

What's more shocking? Lala wondered. The fact that the iconic Dickie Dally turned out to be a waddling, carb-loaded perv? Or that he and Brigitte were still there?

Once they reached the first floor, Brigitte placed her slender arm around Jackson's shoulder. "In Paris, kissing eez like talking. Eez not, how you say...eh...biggie."

"Good to know," Jackson mumbled. And then to Lala, "Now where?"

She fired off a quick text to Clawd asking how everything was going in the gym. He was heading to football practice but assured her that all was well, so she decided to make it her next stop. Besides, they had been everywhere else.

"Ready to check out the gym," Lala said, trying to bring the focus back to the contest. Not that she didn't feel sorry for Jackson, but there would be plenty of time for moping when this was over. Especially if she couldn't find...Frankie!

Finally!

She was running toward them, chasing Cleo down the empty hall. Her hair was a tangled mess, and she was dressed in a—

"Is that green, uh, person wearing a robe?" Dickie asked, his usual bravado dialed down.

"She needs deep condition for zee hairs," Brigitte said, patting her own smooth strands.

Lala was too stunned to respond. Homegirl looked homeless.

"I told you," Cleo shouted, whipping the shoes back at Frankie.

"I don't want them! They're rashy!" The T'eau Dallys smashed into a locker. What the fang was going on? This was like watching fashion week on mute.

"What eez *rashy*?" Brigitte asked Dickie.

"Time out!" Dickie made a T with his hands. "Did anyone see her throw those?"

The floor seemed to shift beneath Lala's feet. With any luck, it would open up and swallow her, making it impossible to see her father's face when he laughed at her colossal failure.

Cleo stormed by. "Stop!" Dickie commanded.

Be nice, Cleo. Be nice.

"'Scuse me?" the royal said.

If Lala had a white flag of surrender, she would have started to wave it.

"You've got quite an arm for a little lady."

Cleo scanned his stained white shirt with disgust and then stared at his third-trimester belly. "And you've got quite a—"

"So!" Lala interjected. "I'd like you to meet—"

Brigitte clutched Frankie's chin and turned it one way and the other. "*Qui a fabriqué vos accessoirs?*" Brigitte pinched the bolts and pulled. "Who makes?"

"Owie!" Frankie swatted the woman's hand away with an audible smack. "That hurts."

"Who eez Zat Hurts? An American designer?" Brigitte asked.

Frankie ran back to retrieve the boots. She stuffed them into Cleo's bag while Dickie was telling her about his grandma Marion, who could pitch a no-hitter while making chutney.

Cleo pulled the boots back out of her bag. "I *said*—"

"Wait!" Frankie leaned forward and whispered something in

her ear. The more she said, the bigger Cleo's smile grew. Her shoulders rolled back, and her chest puffed out.

What is going on?

Lala glared at Jackson, hoping for some insight. He shrugged like someone who couldn't possibly care less.

"Frankie," Lala said, "can I talk to you by the water fountain for a minute?"

"Sure." Frankie smiled.

"What's going on?" Lala hissed. "I've been trying to find you all afternoon! Where's Brett? Why do you look like this? And why are you giving Cleo the shoes? No, wait, why are you *throwing* them?"

Frankie's eyes watered. "I didn't win. It was a miscount. Cleo and Deuce are the real winners."

"*What?!*"

Dickie and Brigitte turned.

Lala lowered her voice. "What are you talking about?"

"High Dam! They pinch!" Cleo shouted, teetering through the hall like someone who'd peed her pants. She had the designer shoes on her feet. "It's like they have teeth."

Just as she was about to fall, Dickie lunged forward and caught her. She swatted his arm like a Nile fly. "Who the *ka* are you, anyway?"

Lala lowered herself to the ground. That way when it opened up, she'd be that much closer to gone.

"Ha!" Dickie's booming voice echoed. He pointed to the TOE DALLY HIGH GYM sign. "Betcha one of those zombies did that."

He slapped his knee. "Gotta use those guys in a helmet commercial. Like, wear a Dally helmet or you might end up brain dead."

Good thing Ghoulia wasn't there. It was also a good thing that he hadn't ruled Merston out. It was a great sign. (Much better than the one he was laughing at.)

But the instant Lala saw the progress, or lack thereof, she began to panic again. Jackson's mural was covered by a splattered drop cloth. Overturned cans of paint flowed toward them like serpents' tongues.

"As soon as Jackson gets back with Deuce, he'll unveil the new T'eau Dally High school crest," Lala said, eager to share something positive. Because Cleo's announcement that she had to go wrap her blisters in linen wasn't quite cutting it. Luckily, Dickie thought she was joking, and Brigitte was struggling through the language barrier. At least the catwalk looked complete. Thank gawd for Clawd.

"In just a few minutes, our It Couple will walk across this stage and model—" *Oh no!* Lala could see the crack in the board. It was still there. Running right down the middle of the plywood.

"Deenie?" Lala called, struggling to sound calm.

Clawdeen scrambled out, barefoot, from under the bleachers. She was wearing the crooked T'eau Dally shorts. And a gray zip-up hoodie that said T'EAU on the left side. Her auburn hair, overgrown and wild, made her look like a wilted sunflower.

Brigitte raised a dark eyebrow and pursed her lips. *"Mon dieu!"* She charged toward Clawdeen like a lion to a gazelle. Clawdeen froze.

"She's fixing it," Lala tried, but it was too late. Brigitte's hands were reaching for Clawdeen's neck.

"Eeez zat real fur?"

Clawdeen nodded, shrinking back.

"What is with French chicks and body hair?" Dickie asked, thumbing through his text messages.

Brigitte stepped forward and tugged. *"Ils sont tellement doux."* She tugged again. "You grow on your skin, *n'est-ce pas?* Like wild bist."

"Clawdeen is a werewolf," Lala said proudly. "I told you about her in my letter. Deenie, this is Brigitte T'eau, from—"

"Isn't she supposed to be here tomorrow?"

"Yes, they showed up a day early and are making my life miserable," Lala whispered in a way that only Clawdeen and her super ears could hear. "Please just go with this. It's our only chance."

Clawdeen rolled her yellow-brown eyes in a *you-owe-me* sort of way.

Lala nodded. *I promise.*

Brigitte pulled nail clippers from her bag and snipped off a sample as Clawdeen whimpered. "Weel do a whole weenter boots line with theez furs. We call them Outer Were, like Werewolf, *non?"*

"Non," Clawdeen growled. It was a good thing her overprotective brothers weren't around to hear this.

"Um, actually, Ms. T'eau, real fur isn't popular here," Lala said.

Brigitte threw back her head and laughed. *"Mais, non!"*

"Same thing with leather. But your faux looks T'eau-tally awesome." She tried softening the blow by referencing Brigitte's fake-leather tank and leather pants.

209

"*Faux?*" Brigitte gasped. "Deez is not faux! I say *non* to faux."

Lala and Clawdeen exchanged a glance. "But your shoes. The new co-design. The straps are synthetic, right?"

"Synthetic? Ha!" Dickie said, dropping his phone back in its holster. "Our shoes are made from kangaroo."

What?!

"Real kangaroo?"

"Just zee *bébé*," Brigitte said. "How you say, *jolie*?"

"Joey," Dickie corrected her.

Lala's pulse began to hop. They had to be joking.

"Touch," he said, offering his tan wallet. "One hundred percent joey hide. Soft and durable. My 2015 line of jockstraps will be made of the stuff. A wonder for down under. Ha! How's that for a slogan?"

Cleo appeared before them, flanked by Blue and Frankie, who were helping her stay upright in the shoes. "Nothing a little oil and linen can't fix," she said. "By the time they get here tomorrow, I'll be shooting hoops in these bear traps." Lala took that moment to make the introductions. Cleo's tanned skin blanched when she realized what she had been saying. Frankie sparked. Blue kept mouthing *what?* in search of an explanation.

"Ha! Bear traps," Dickie swatted Brigitte on the arm like a teammate. "Hear that? That could be next. Sandals made of bear. You know, they hibernate during the winter."

"We can put bolts on zee sides, like claws," Brigitte riffed. "And what are zees?" she asked, rubbing her finger along Frankie's wrist seams. "Zay are zo silky."

"Real bear?" Frankie asked, hiding her hands in the pockets of her robe.

"*Mais oui*," Brigitte said proudly. "Just like zee kangaroo."

"Kangaroo?" Blue asked, eyeing Lala. "Is this sheila fair dinkum?"

Lala nodded, her insides churning as though she'd just eaten lamb.

"Nothing but the best," boasted Dickie. He pointed at Cleo's feet. "Those shoes right there were tested on monkeys."

"Monkeys?" Clawdeen barked.

"Two dozen," he announced. "We ran 'em on treadmills for three hours. That joey didn't even so much as crack."

"Joey!" Blue said, her eyes filling with tears.

"*Ka!*" Cleo said, kicking off the shoes.

"Don't hurt it," Blue said, running to retrieve them.

Brigitte smiled, thinking Blue loved the line. "Perhaps zee scaly one should be our model."

"Her?" Cleo gasped, grabbing the shoes.

"Take 'em, mate," Blue said. "S'not enough moolah in lucky country to get me in those."

All fears of her father's *I-told-you-so* faded to the back of Lala's reeling mind. Pushed aside by images of high-heeled monkeys on treadmills. Skinned roos. Plucked bolts. Wolf-fur boots.

The girls looked at Lala, silently urging her to do something. She was about to ask if it was too late to change the shoe design, when Deuce appeared with Jackson and Heath.

He kissed Cleo hello and asked, "What's with that thing on your foot? Did you have surgery or something?"

"No, but I'll need it if I have to wear these shoes for one more second."

"Tell me who makes your skin cleaning and I should forget I heard zat," Brigitte said.

"Why, so you can turn me into a handbag?"

"Ha!" Dickie laughed.

Cleo looked at her boyfriend, hoping he'd punch Dickie and defend her honor. But instead he held out his hand and said, "Mr. Dally, I love your basketball gear."

To which Dickie responded, "And I love your taste in broads." Deuce dropped his hand in shock.

"How about we unveil the mural?" Jackson said, leading the group toward the giant drop cloth. Jackson grabbed one corner and waited while Heath took a final sip from his forty-two-ounce Super Big Gulp and grabbed another corner.

"It's not quite done," Jackson explained. "But you'll get the idea."

"One…two…three!" Heath said. They tugged the giant cloth. It snapped and billowed and then *brraaaaap!* Heath's Big Gulp became a big burp. An enormous fireball shot through the air and landed directly in the middle of the billowing sheet, immediately engulfing the fabric in flickering orange flames.

"Ahhhhh!" screamed Jackson, fearing the heat. He threw the sheet onto the plywood stage. Seconds later it began to burn. Crackling embers popped and soared throughout the gym, setting fire to the river of paint that snaked along the floor.

Wooop-wooop-wooop. The fire alarm began to ring. Sprinklers lowered from the ceiling, spraying frigid water across the gym. Blue began dancing in the mist while everyone else fanned away the smoke and searched for the exit.

Frankie began sparking. "Code green!"

"*Zut alors, mes cheveux!*" Brigitte shouted. "It frizzez in zee rain."

"Maybe we can make a loofah out of it," Lala said.

"*Pardonnez-moi?*"

"Yeah, we can turn your hair into a loofah and use your bony arms as coffee stirrers," she shouted, no longer fearing her father's disapproval. *Who cares about college applications?* She had thousands of years ahead of her. She'd do something worth touting eventually. Right now she wanted to stand up for what she believed in. Like animal safety. Like the rights of RADs. Like herself. It might not serve Merston High, but there was more to life than school, especially when life was forever.

Fire trucks wailed in the distance. Hurried feet rushed down the hallway as classes emptied and students ran for the parking lot. Haylee appeared through the smoke, blasting her emergency fire extinguisher like an Uzi.

The lights in the gym flickered. Heath bolted for the exit. Shivering, Lala lifted her face to the cold water, inviting it to wash away the sticky, dirty feeling that had been plaguing her like a bad case of dysentery all afternoon.

The red emergency-lighting system kicked in, bathing the gym in a devilish glow. Just in time to illuminate Dickie as he body-slammed into Deuce, knocking the Gorgon's sunglasses to the floor. He covered his eyes. "My glasses! Somebody, get my glasses!"

Crunch!

Dickie's white tennis shoe crash-landed on the frames. Deuce's eyes popped open. Dickie began to slip.

"Ahhh—" His scream was cut short. A round stone sculpture appeared on the floor in his place.

213

Deuce covered his eyes again. "Get me out of here!"

"I've got you," Lala said, racing to his side. "I can see in the dark, don't worry."

"Can you lead me out of here?" he asked.

"On one condition," Lala said.

"What?" He coughed.

"Open your eyes."

CHAPTER TWENTY-FIVE
FRANKIE DOODLE DANDY

"Sadie Warlock...Su-Chin Weinstein...Brandon White..."
Principal Weeks's voice was amplified across the campus. One by
one, he called the graduates to the outdoor stage to receive their
diplomas. The closer he got to the end of the alphabet, the closer
the Merston senior class was to freedom. And the closer Frankie
was to showtime.

"He's on *W*," Frankie announced to her team. "We've got no
*X*s, four *Y*s, and one *Z*. We're at T minus five. I'm taking my final
walk-through."

The members of the Balance Board stood proudly by their
posts, awaiting inspection. But a quick glance was all Frankie
needed. It was perfect.

What had once been a quaint school courtyard was now a
work of art. As if sculpted over centuries, the maple trees, the
brick walls, and the cobblestone pavers were coated in smooth
white stone. The creeping ivy was stone. The tulips were stone.
And the round garden tables were stone. While escaping the fire,

Deuce (with a little encouragement from Lala) had transformed the entire school into what looked like a scene from *The Flintstones*. (Well, okay, Deuce started it, but a formidable decor maven was called in to finish the job—namely, Deuce's mom. But she let him take the credit.)

Lockers were impossible to open. Backpacks too dense to lift. And instead of "Pomp and Circumstance," graduates walked to the tune of jackhammers and bulldozers. There was something about students fighting to move past the old beliefs, only to get thrown back into the Stone Age, that struck Frankie as funny... or poetic...or was it ironic? Maybe it was existential? Whatever it was, it was mint, and worth pointing out.

So when Haylee called last night at 11:46 PM, crying because she couldn't make her "We Are the World" theme work in a rock garden, Frankie sparked into action. She wanted something that summed up the year. Something that said life is not black and white. Sometimes it's green. She wanted to work with what she had been given, not fight to change it. She wanted to accept. Because wasn't that what the past year had been all about?

And so "Stoned High: A Graphite Novel" was created. Written with sidewalk chalk on every tree, brick, and boulder in the courtyard, the colorful illustrations and graffiti-like text documented the most memorable moments of the year. Ghoulia was in charge of chalk. Jackson illustrated. Brett, Heath, and Irish Emmy were shooting video, and Haylee would greet the guests and guide them to the buffet table. The task was beneath her, but Haylee clearly needed a break from the pressure, and so did her blotchy complexion.

"And, finally, Moan'ica Yelps," said Principal Weeks.

216

"Y a y y y," Ghoulia groaned for her older sister.

An orchestra of jackhammers blasted as the graduates tossed their caps in the air. And then, black gowns soaring behind them, they descended on the luncheon like a colony of bats.

"Here they come!" Frankie called.

"Thank you," Haylee said, her beige glasses misting.

"For what?"

"You saved me." Haylee looked around. "You saved the luncheon. And it looks sooo—" She paused to blow her nose.

Frankie put her hand on Haylee's shoulder pad. "I know what it feels like to have an entire school blame you for things. And I wouldn't wish that on—" She paused. "Hey, can I ask you something?"

Haylee nodded.

"Why did you give Cleo your speech?"

Haylee pressed the tissue to her nose. "She gave me this." She lifted the blue eye charm on her necklace.

"The Eye of Horus?" Frankie could hardly contain her shock. Maybe Haylee wasn't so smart after all. "You can get those in every gift shop east of Hungary."

Haylee giggled. "She said it's a twenty-twenty amulet, you know, to help my vision."

Frankie gasped. "And you *believed* her?"

Haylee giggled. " 'Course not. But I've been taking glassblowing classes after school. Heath and I want to make vases this summer and sell them at art festivals. The most expensive part is the furnace, and Heath can do that, so... Anyway, with school, and glassblowing, and the luncheon, and my dog-walking business, the contest was just too much. I needed an excuse to quit."

217

She lifted her glasses and pinched the moistening corners of her eyes. "Sorry. I think I'm just really burned out."

Frankie pulled her in for a hug. "It's okay."

"Are we going to stay in touch next year?" Haylee sniffled.

"Of course," Frankie said. "I'm going to need you to watch Brett for me."

"And you'll watch Heath at Radcliffe?"

Frankie made an X across her ivory eyelet maxidress. "Cross my bolts and hope to fry."

"Here they come." Haylee smiled. "I'd better go greet."

Frankie waved good-bye and then snapped one last picture of the courtyard. Vibrant and sentimental, the chalk drawings told a story of triumph. The story began with an image of Brett screaming at the Monster Mash dance as he held Frankie's fallen head in his hands. In the middle it showed Frankie interviewing RADs for the "Ghoul Next Door" video. At the end was Mrs. Foose's rainbow. It was a story, Frankie finally realized, that couldn't have been told without her. Because in the sky, above the rainbow, was a green star. That star was Frankie.

A floating stone tulip stopped in front of Frankie. "This was your idea?"

"Why does everyone sound so surprised?" she asked, no longer taking it as a compliment.

"It's just so..." Billy struggled to find a word that wouldn't offend her.

"Voltage?"

"Yeah, voltage." He handed her the tulip.

"What's this for?"

"I'm sorry."

"For what? Switching the ballot boxes because you thought I couldn't win? Or not thinking I could come up with a cool luncheon theme?"

"Both."

Frankie took the flower and twirled it between her fingers. "How'd you know I wouldn't win?"

"Because, my dear"—Billy gripped her shoulders—"your speech sucked."

Frankie burst out laughing and pulled her invisible friend in for a hug. It could not have looked normal.

"Either that's InvisiBilly or you're in one crazy game of freeze tag," said Candace Carver. She was the only graduate who'd belted her gown and had her initials—CC—sewn onto the back to look like the Chanel logo. "Great luncheon, by the way."

"Where's Melody?" Frankie asked.

"She took off after the ceremony. Something about the band or Jackson. I dunno. Listening to her can be dangerous. Anyway, B, my parents just surprised me with a first-class ticket. Coach class out!"

"Where are you going?" Frankie asked.

"I'm going to France for the summer to observe street fashion. Billy and Spectra are coming with me, since, you know, they can fly for free."

Frankie sparked. She looked at Billy. *Thanks for telling me.*

"I was gonna say something," he said, seeing Frankie's fireworks. "But you weren't exactly taking my calls the last few days."

219

"Since when do you bother calling?" Frankie teased, hugging him again.

"Candace? Is that you?" asked a dark-haired babe in a tweed blazer as he pushed his way toward them.

Can's green eyes widened. Frankie had never seen a normie look so shocked.

"Shane?" She finger-fluffed her curls. "Um, what are you doing here?"

Shane crossed his arms. "My sister Mindy just graduated."

Candace twirled a blond curl. "You're Mindy's *brother*?"

Shane lifted an eyebrow and nodded. "And you're in high school."

Candace lifted her glass of lemonade and winked. "College now."

Shane knocked the glass from her hand and stormed away.

Hundreds of eyes turned to see how Candace Carver would react to being dumped. Not that she noticed. She was too busy scanning her iPhone for her France to-do list. "Number one," she read. "Cut all ties with American boys." She swiped the screen and tapped Delete. "Shane *out*."

Frankie pulled off her plum gladiator sandals and sat on a stone bush. She wiggled her green toes and waited for Brett to finish packing up the sound equipment.

Principal Weeks walked toward her, arm extended.

"Wonderful job, Miss Stein!" he said, shaking her hand. "I hope you're planning on running for the council next year."

Frankie sighed. "I think so. But it looks like I'll be doing it at Radcliffe."

The principal's narrow shoulders slumped at least four inches. "Ah, Radcliffe. The dagger in the heart of my career." He loosened his tie, which said *Happy Graduation* in nine different languages.

Frankie sniffed. "I thought *we* were the dagger."

"The students?"

"No, the RADs."

Weeks's sharp blue eyes met hers. "I've always known this community was special. But I had to respect the wishes of your parents and keep things quiet. Nothing has thrilled me more than seeing you kids come together and stand up for what's right." He pulled a red bandanna out of his wrinkled beige suit pocket and dabbed his beading forehead. "And now you'll all be gone...."

Frankie's heart space caved in a little. She couldn't imagine it either. "What's going to happen to this place?"

"Trailers," he said, looking at the rubble piles that dotted the campus like giant anthills. "Until we rebuild. But we will. We're survivors. Just like you." He smiled. "Who knows? Maybe you'll change your mind and stay."

"I love Merston and all." Frankie stood and patted his rounded shoulder. "But trailer classrooms? So not mint."

CHAPTER TWENTY-SIX
OVER THE RAINBOW

"Leopard tank. Middle closet between the zebra leggings and cheetah mini. Stat!" Candace instructed.

Melody slid the mirrored doors to the right. "The large or the small?"

Candace whipped off her white cat-eye sunglasses and glared. *What do you think?*

"Small it is."

Candace snatched it up, rolled it into the size of a Tic Tac, and stuffed it into the army-green duffel.

Melody peeked out at the white cottage across the street. Jackson's window was open. His curtains swayed. Melody's heart jumped. Had he skipped the Camp Crescendo orientation to see her off? The curtains swayed again. *Just the wind.*

"We're working here!" Candace snapped her fingers. "Black jeggings. Zippers at the ankles. In the pants closet, skinny side."

Melody tucked the pants next to the denim vest. Something winked at her from the bottom of the bag. "A sequin bustier?"

Candace was standing in front of her mirror, contemplating a black fedora. "When sequins call, you'd better answer. And, trust me, they call at the oddest of times." She tossed the fedora out the window like last summer's Frisbee. "In less than twenty-four hours, I'm going to be eating chocolate croissants in a bistro, speaking Fransay to hot garsawns."

Melody sighed, collapsing onto the pink frilly bed. "I need to take five." She hugged a white satin pillow to her chest and squeezed.

Candace lay down beside her sister. She pulled a feather from Melody's hair. "I'm gonna miss you, freak." She hugged Melody. Hard.

Melody breathed in Candace's Black Orchid perfume. Maybe if she inhaled deeply enough, the smell would stay with her until August. "No good-byes, remember?"

Candace sniff-nodded. Was she thinking about the last ten months too? The months that made them close in a way the previous fifteen years never had? The move to Oregon? The day they met Jackson? The day they saw Jackson turn into Hyde? Cofounding NUDI? Realizing they weren't blood sisters? Deciding that it didn't matter?

Melody propped herself up on her elbow and looked at Candace's glitter-covered eyelids. "Every day, no matter where you are, you're going to find an Internet café and update me on what you're doing." Candace began to blink rapidly. "I want details. Pictures. And the truth."

"Lying out," Candace agreed, spellbound.

Siren 1, normie 0.

Hissssssssss. They heard the sound of brakes outside.

Melody and Candace froze. *This is it. One…two…three…* Melody jumped to the sheepskin rug and buried her unpolished toes into the fur.

"Your ride is here!" Glory called from downstairs.

Candace zipped the duffel and shoved it toward Melody. "If you don't become a rock icon with this wardrobe, you're dead to me."

Glory and Beau were waiting for her by the front door, sobbing.

"I'll see you tomorrow night in Seattle," Melody said. "And then in Portland, and San Francisco, and Anaheim, and San Diego." Still, she swallowed a horse-pill-sized urge to cry. Even though her parents would be at every show, and trailing the bus with their equipment, this was the end of an era. Melody was stepping out for the first time. Her world would never be small again—her burgeoning talent would see to that. Like a racehorse, it needed practice to reach its potential. Space to hit its stride. Salem was too small for that. Every step she took toward her future meant a step farther from her past.

Beau ruffled his daughter's already messy hair. "Don't drink."

"Don't do drugs," Glory added.

"And no hoodies!" Candace called from upstairs, refusing to have her eyes leak in public.

They laughed and hugged. They exchanged kisses. *I'll miss you*s. They promised to hit the road after they dropped Candace off at the airport. They were a family sending Melody off to join a new one. They were proof that letting someone go is the ultimate show of love—something Jackson obviously wasn't willing to do.

The doors of the burgundy tour bus hissed open, sharing the shrill intro to "Paradise City" with the humid afternoon.

Granite dashed out. "I'll get that," he said, reaching for her luggage. But Melody continued dragging her duffel bag down the steps as if it were a corpse.

"You're a manager now," she teased. "Can't you have the roadie do it?"

He grabbed the bag and hoisted it over his shoulder. It reminded Melody of the night they met, when he rescued her from the dance floor. "Yeah, well, until we fill that position, I'm kind of both."

"I'll have to talk to my buddy Lew about that."

"Please do," he said, heaving the bag into the side hatch at the base of the bus. "Ready?" He smiled like someone with a surprise. But Melody knew he was trying to control his excitement. Trying to stay cool. Trying not to climb onto the roof of the bus and shout, "We're going on tour!" She knew because her insides were slam dancing too.

"Welcome aboard!" Nine-Point-Five shouted over Guns N' Roses. She and Cici were standing on the black leather couches taping Leadfeather posters to the wood-veneer cabinets. Sage was putting a new plastic Christmas tree together, its skinny branches ready to accept donations from friends they had yet to meet. The bus smelled like a mix of leather and candy—a scent Melody would come to associate with beginning.

Beyond the couches and kitchenette were six bunk beds. Three on each side, they looked more like the shelves in Candace's closet. Decadent for a walk-in, perfectly no-frills for rock and roll. Behind the bunks was a phone booth–sized bathroom and shower. And behind that were two Bose speakers. It was perfect.

"Ready?" Granite called, starting the engine. As well as manager and roadie, he was their driver.

"Ready!" the band members called.

Melody pushed open the window and blew kisses to her family as they waved and blew kisses back. She turned to look at Jackson's house one last time, just in case. But like all the other times, he was gone.

As the bus began rolling, Sage doled out the chocolate milk. "To Leadfeather!"

"To Leadfeather!" her bandmates answered, knocking cartons and then guzzling.

Granite turned onto I-5 north. No longer just a freeway, it was now a road paved with endless possibility.

"Say good-bye to Salem," Cici called.

Sage and Nine-Point-Five clambered onto the sofas and waved. But not Melody. She moved up front and sat beside Granite. She vowed never to look back again.

And then her phone rang.

The number was Jackson's but the voice—lively and amped—was D.J.'s. "No chance you're hitting the road without me," he said, guitar blaring in the background.

Melody laughed—one part surprise, two parts relief. Jackson hadn't abandoned her; he'd abandoned himself. For her. It was the ultimate sacrifice. It was love. It was awesome.

"We do need a roadie," Melody said. "The money is terrible, and the food is worse."

"I'll take it!" D.J. texted his location, and the tour bus turned around. It was the perfect end of one story and the ultimate beginning of another. Smellody out.

EPILOGUE
RAD TO THE BONE

TUESDAY, SEPTEMBER 2

The maple trees had been replanted to form an arch. From above, the fall leaves—red, yellow, green, orange, and brown—looked like a pixelated rainbow. The redwood-and-glass building at the end of the arch, a pot of gold.

At least that's how it appeared in the photograph that hung above the entrance.

Mr. D, dressed in faded jeans and an untucked black button-down, was standing in front of the satin ribbon that stretched across the glass like gift wrapping. Lala stood beside him, twirling a parasol in one hand and holding gold scissors in the other. Count Fabulous was perched on her shoulder wearing a pink-and-black-striped sleep mask and his new back-to-school tiara.

"Welcome to..." Her father tugged a rope, and a pink-and-black banner unfurled. The crowd gasped. *Radcliffe* was not the name inside the school's crest. Thanks to Lala's urgings, it had been changed to something more meaningful. Something that would remind its students of the night that started everything—the night Frankie Stein lost her head. The night she exposed the RADs. The night normies reordered the letters on the Merston High sign. The night that marked the beginning of the end.

"Welcome to Monster High," Mr. D said to the hundreds facing them. "The most state-of-the-art educational facility in the country!"

Applause.

"I could spend all afternoon telling you about the acres of land we have made available to our athletes, the portable charging stations, the fountain desks and water lanes, the stone-melting tools, the accessory and clothing design electives, the modern mummy classes, the air-conditioning fedoras, the portable heat lamps, our music program, our animal rescue shelter and grooming spa..."

Lala beamed. Count Fabulous flapped his wings.

"...but I'll let you see them for yourselves."

"Woooo-hoooo!" someone cheered.

Mr. D held up his palm. "But first there are several people I need to thank." He looked out at the crowd and smiled.

Smiled!

"Ram de Nile for funding the project (*applause*) and the Wolfs for their remarkable construction (*applause*). The Steins, Ms. J, and our new voice teacher, Marina, for developing a challenging and nontraditional curriculum that also fulfills all of Oregon's state standards (*applause*). Mr. Weeks for agreeing to serve as principal (*applause*). Deuce Gorgon and Clawd Wolf for convincing the Oregon Sports Organization to recognize our teams (*massive applause*). And..." Mr. D took off his sunglasses. He squinted into the sun and then put his arm around his daughter. His touch warmed her in a way that Clawd and cashmere never could. "Most of all, my remarkable daughter Lala and her electrifying friend Frankie Stein. I don't know many girls who would spend their summer persuading me to open up your school to normies. But they did. And so I have (*enormous applause*). And I assure you they did it without the help of Sirens." Melody and Jackson laughed. "So without further ado, I give you...Monster High!"

Deafening applause.

The Wolfs covered their ears while Lala leaned forward and cut the ribbon. Everyone charged forward.

Lala watched the stampede but didn't join in. Her father's arm was still around her. She was close enough to smell his self-tanner. For some reason, he wasn't rushing off either. Lala wanted to savor this moment as long as she possibly could.

"Did you really mean that?" she asked, looking up at his strong jaw.

He gazed at her. His black eyes looked more like shiny pearls than stones. "Mean what?"

Lala considered making something up. She was still afraid to show him how much she wanted his approval. Not for fear of what he would do, but rather for fear of what he wouldn't. Trusting him with her feelings would take time. But she finally trusted herself. And she knew that no matter how he reacted to the things she said or did, she'd survive. She might even thrive.

"Did you mean that I'm remarkable?" she pressed. "Do you really think that?"

"One of the most remarkable women I know," he said, and

then looked sadly at something far beyond the trees. "I don't say it very often, do I?"

"Um, I can count on one fang how many times you've said it."

He chuckled once without smiling. "I guess I always assumed you knew."

Lala pulled herself out from under his grasp, the tender moment broken like a spell. "Why would I assume that?" Her hands began to shake. She popped an iron pill and swallowed it without water. It stuck to the back of her throat, like so many things she wanted to say but never could. "Dad." She swallowed again. *Bite by bite*... "We communicate by satellite. You live on a boat and talk to a headset. Your take more pride in your tan than your own family. You freak out my pets!" She forced herself to face him. He was looking at his polished black shoes. "Maybe it's because I don't eat meat, or I'm dating a Wolf, or I agree with Uncle Vlad that our house would look cool with a splash of color. But whatever it is, I—"

"It's your mother!" he snapped, fangs bared.

Huh?

"Laura," he said, using the name her mother had given her. "Do you have any idea how much you look like her?"

Lala showed him her fangs in an indignant attempt to prove otherwise. She regretted it immediately.

"You have her fire. You are the only woman who challenges me the way she did. The only person. You make me question the things I believe in. You take the black and white out of things and try to add...pink."

"What's wrong with that?"

"Color is unpredictable," he said, as if admitting something more.

"Like normie death?" Lala asked, catching on.

He nodded. "Like the pain of losing someone you love to something you will never understand."

Lala stood on her tiptoes and kissed him on the cheek. "You won't lose me."

"I'm afraid I already have," he said, his eyes beginning to water.

She fang-poked his arm. "So the first one thousand five hundred and ninety-nine years were a little rocky. It's nothing we can't fix."

Her father sniffle-laughed and pulled her close. "Remarkable."

Arm in arm, they crossed the threshold to Monster High and joined the others. They looked like every other father and daughter. It was *fang-tastic*!

ACKNOWLEDGMENTS

A very voltage thanks to my editor, Erin Stein.*
Your genius and enthusiasm keep me sparking.

XXXXX Lisi

*Turns out, she's a bolt relative of Frankie's.**
Get it? Frankie Stein? Erin Stein?*
Bolt relative? Blood relative?*
****...Forget it.